Death in Chicago

D1531207

DEATH IN CHICAGO: WINTER
by Dominic J. Grassi

Edited by Michael Coyne and Gregory F. Augustine Pierce
Cover design by Hugh Spector
Text design and typesetting by Patricia A. Lynch

Copyright © 2018 by Dominic J. Grassi

Published by In Extenso Press
Distributed exclusively by ACTA Publications, 4848 N. Clark Street,
Chicago, IL 60640, (800) 397-2282, actapublications.com

Library of Congress Catalog Number: 2017962388
ISBN: 978-0-87946-976-4 (paperback)
ISBN: 978-0-87946-975-7 (hardcover)
Printed in the United States of America by Total Printing Systems
Year 30 29 28 27 26 25 24 23 22 21 20 19 18
Printing 15 14 13 12 11 10 9 8 7 6 5 4 3 2

♻ Text printed on 30% post-consumer recycled paper

Death in Chicago

WINTER

DOMINIC J. GRASSI

i.e.

in extenso

CHAPTER ONE

Somebody once said, maybe it was Jerry Garcia, that what we ultimately become is nothing more nor less than a reflection of the choices we have made in life. We don't get to decide just once who or what we want to be: tinker, tailor, soldier, priest. We choose again and again, in each unfolding moment, and have to live with the consequences of those choices forever. Pondering that fact in a dark and favorite bar in the middle of the afternoon on the far North Side of Chicago, I am finding it no wonder that my life is such a mess on this bleak February day in 2009, late in what has been a typically hard winter. Approaching my sixth decade, I am counting heavily right now on my one and only friend, Jack, surnamed Daniels, Black Label, of course. I find myself calling on him more and more these days.

I'm waiting for one Ed Waterman in the dim light of a sticky booth near the back of the room. Two o'clock, he said, anywhere I wanted. I could have picked a place closer to home, but I chose St. Martin's Inn in Edgewater because it is the seediest of the bars I am known to frequent. And that's saying a lot. I can't even imagine there being a bar in his home town of Wilmette. That old-money North Shore suburb probably doesn't allow bars on its BMW-lined streets. And if they do, they sure don't smell like this trap. The odors of spilled beer, unwashed bodies, and pine-scented urinal cakes all blend together in an all-too-familiar air that somehow comforts and assures regular denizens of the dark like me. I've already stolen a little head start on Waterman. I've been here since noon and Jack's first stop at my table was a quick one. "First one fast" is a policy that just never seems to fail me. His second visit was more leisurely. I'm nursing this third glass now and starting to feel comfortably numb. That's what a good friend will do for you, put the world at arm's length and give you a moment of serenity. A moment of sweet oblivion. But even the whiskey has faltered at softening the ragged edge of tension grinding at me in recent weeks. Lately even Jack can't seem to keep the adrenaline from squirting through me for no apparent reason. So I'm stuck with a sense of dread that even Old No. 7 can't cover up today. Having to meet with Ed Waterman is helping not one bit.

Waterman. I hadn't seen him since May of 1976. May 11, to be exact. That was the day he had me kicked out of St. Mary of the Lake Seminary in Mundelein, the "Enchanted Forest" to those select men and boys privileged to live there. It was the week before I was scheduled to be ordained a deacon, a year before my long-striven-for ordination to the priesthood. In those candidate-rich days of Holy Mother Church, the Archdiocese of Chicago could still afford to be choosey in discerning whom the Holy Spirit really wanted to see elevated to priesthood. My name got swiped from the list.

One of my classmates, I never figured out who, turned me in for taking a buzz as I sat alone on the pier erected by the very Cardinal Mundelein whose name the town bears. I was caught toking while watching an historically spectacular spring storm cross St. Mary's Lake. It was a religious experience, a moment of communion with God's created world, is how I tried to sell it to then Fr. Edward Waterman, Dean of Formation, who wasn't buying. He sported a crisp crew cut, spit-shined wingtips, and a perfect manicure, and reeked, as always, of bay rum aftershave and the odor of his own sanctity. I couldn't shake the feeling that he relished canning a bad apple like me. In a way I had just become his newly elected golden boy, I was his cherished bad example.

What we might call today a cautionary tale. When word of my canning got out, not a few of my classmates got haircuts, flushed their secret stash down the toilets in the seminary bathrooms, and had their new and better moment of come-to-Jesus.

The irony of the fact that Waterman would leave the priesthood in disgrace six weeks later did not escape me. He ran off with a doe-eyed girl, a recent graduate of Barat College, the exclusive school for good Catholic girls just down the road in Lake Forest. Seems that throughout her senior year they were doing the old down-and-dirty behind the ample backs of the oblivious Madams of the Sacred Heart. In any case, the good father ignored my pleas that day and I was cast from Mundelein as unceremoniously as Satan was cast from the right hand of God. So I left behind the first estate and set out afresh to seek my rightful place in the world.

One of the funny things about having a religious vocation is that you never get to be fifteen. While all my boyhood friends were launching their adolescent voyages of self-discovery, I was closeted in my bedroom translating Caesar's *The Gallic Wars* from the original Latin. In the seminary, you're so focused on achieving your dream that you never get to be that young adult with your whole life in front of you and no responsibility in the world beyond securing your own temporal satisfaction. So I decided that's what I ought to do, and then I went and did it. For the next ten years. I drifted west and dropped out. I panhandled. I picked lettuce with migrants who possessed not a dozen words of English among them. Sold magazine subscriptions. Worked the window at an all-night taco trailer. Held a short gig as a bonded security guard in a chilled Embarcadero warehouse on the graveyard shift, making sure nobody snuck in and stole the bananas ripening there. Peddled a little blotter acid out the back door of Buddy's Quick Stop in Hunter's Point.

I did almost manage to hang on to one sure thing, Peggy

Hackett, a Chicago girl with violet eyes to die for, who hitched her wagon to my star for a while and followed me when I struck west. She tried her best to get me to grow up, but couldn't in the end. I came home from work one morning to an empty apartment in Sausalito with my unfolded clothes in a heap in the middle of the living room floor. "Gone home," was all the note on the floor next to my clothes said. She took the pen with her. I added her name to the long list of people I have disappointed in my life and moved on.

I never managed to stay anywhere or with anyone for long after Peggy. I burned a lot of hemp and burnt out more than a few girlfriends. I lost touch with my family. Never heard about my father's death until three months after he was in the ground. The years passed. Some of them are just gone to me now. I finally figured I'd had enough of being fifteen and walked out to the I-80 ramp one morning carrying an army surplus duffle bag filled with all my worldly goods and a cardboard sign that read "Chicago or Bust" and never once looked back.

I got home seven days later. Slept in my old room with Mom's blessing. Cut my hair a little shorter. Stopped smoking up, usually. Started taking criminal justice courses at Truman College and began to study Tae Kwon Do to get myself in shape. I never did muster the courage to look Peggy Hackett up.

After a while I took a notion to join the Chicago police force, maybe even become a detective. You'd be surprised at the number of guys in the seminary who at one time or another found themselves torn between the cops and the cassock. I think it must have something to do with needing to be the one in charge. But a couple of minor legal scrapes from my days in the wild, wild west kept me from qualifying.

"You could still be a private eye," one of my old seminary buddies, who is in fact a city detective, offered one day when I was down in the dumps. "All you got to do is take the test. They give you a manual and everything. You can answer wrong like 30% of the time and you still get a pass. I know lots worse degenerates than you with a private peeper's license."

So that's what I did.

To meet the requirements for qualifying experience, I may have embellished my gig as a security guard, both in terms of its longevity and the paramount importance of my duties, which mainly entailed not falling asleep if a boss was around and not stealing too many green bananas yourself. But eight months, two tests, and $600 later I put out my own shingle. "Cosmo Grande," my name, "Confidential Investigations," and my phone number are all that is written on my business card.

I rented a tiny second floor walk-up, as cheap as I could find, in an art deco limestone building at Clark and Diversey that looks like it is right out of the 1940s. No receptionist, no name hand-painted on the door in block letters, no tenor sax blaring *Blue Seven* as I walk toward it down the dark, rain-washed streets of the second city that never sleeps. But an office nonetheless. A place of my own. A reflection of the choices I have made in my life. I mainly expose unfaithful husbands and trace deadbeat dads. I often see the same guy more than once. I go to a lot of ugly divorce proceedings and give sworn testimony that somehow always casts the most favorable light on people who have given me a little money. I drew my gun once to shoo a mugger, but mainly use it to keep papers from blowing around on my desk in spring and fall when the windows are open. I don't have to put the Tae Kwon Do to use all that often, but I do enjoy teasing a little blood from the nose of an occasional wife beater who I find particularly annoying. I've got a cartoon taped to the wall behind my desk. Two guys in hair-shirts are hanging in chains from the dark stone wall of a medieval dungeon. One is turned to the other and he's saying, "It's a living."

My record is clean. I never work on Sundays. Usually I eat

my plate of Sunday pasta all alone in my underwear with the television on. Prego isn't half bad. I will admit that I keep looking for a woman with violet eyes and legs this long and a dead mother and a doll-faced Persian cat to finally sweep me off my flattened feet. It hasn't happened so far. I've been living a mainly celibate life, not so much out of virtue, but probably as more of a regular habit than a lot of my ordained classmates. You don't need a P.I. license to figure that out.

I'm starting to worry about myself a little lately. I wonder, am I slipping? Or is it just the weed that I've started using again to mellow me out at the end of a long day? It is actually easier to procure than ever, more potent, and while it isn't exactly cheap, it's a lot cheaper than in the old days. But no matter how slow business is, I always find a way to have my buddy Jack at my side. There is some talk on the streets that I have started to get a little too rough with some of the people my clients have asked me to maneuver into a state of compliance. People just seem to piss me off lately. I don't know, maybe I've just been angry so long that I've forgotten why.

═══

So I'm sitting here alone in St. Martin's, waiting for a ghost from my storied past to appear. There's just a little Jack left sitting in the melting cubes. I give the glass one last lift. Someone walks in and from the way he screws up his face as he takes the dive in I know that it must be Ed Waterman of the Waterman Family Furniture Stores. I look at my watch. Two o'clock on the dot. I wait for his eyes to meet mine. He glances over at me and then looks past like he doesn't recognize me. I lift my empty glass in a toast and he starts to walk toward me. A chilling draft from the door he opened follows right behind him.

CHAPTER TWO

Grande?"

"Have a seat."

"Christ, Grande. What kind of dump have you dragged me into?"

Some things will never change. He's still the Dean of Students, still enjoys passing judgment. He still carries himself like a drill instructor, but seems to have lost his tall-man's confidence, and looks like a man the years have taken a toll on. I can see a little spot of whisker he missed on his chin this morning, and a fleck of congealed blood low on his neck. His hair is all silver now, but still cut in the high fade he favored in 1972.

"Sorry, I don't do Wilmette. What are you drinking?" I ask as I lift my empty glass to get Marge's attention at the bar. "Marge will fix you up with whatever you need. The premier selection of top-shelf libations here is rivaled only by the décor."

Waterman makes a tight gesture with his mouth that isn't exactly a grimace, but isn't exactly a smile either. He looks over to the general area where Marge is standing, but not directly at her.

"Johnny Walker Red. Make it a double, one ice cube. Not two. One." He lifts and shakes an upright index finger as if at heaven above.

I notice the slight arching of Marge's eyebrows. Waterman is oblivious to it. Marge pours and saunters over with the two drinks. The good thing about Marge, no matter what else you say about her, is that she pours them deep. God bless the bartender who counts slow. Now Jack and Johnny are meeting together.

That's always nice. She sets the glasses down on chipboard coasters with retro nudie cartoons from the 1950s printed on them. Waterman's hand shakes a little as he reaches for his drink.

I see this a lot. Nobody ever looks me up because everything's going so rosy. But a rattled client doesn't usually tell me the things I need to know. I think it best to try to relax him a bit. Also to give Johnny Walker a moment to do his job.

"You're looking good, Ed."

I very consciously use his first name. It works a little. He tries to force another smile but it comes out more like a series of twitches.

"Thanks, Cosmo, you haven't changed much yourself."

"I haven't changed much in over thirty years? Are you a liar or are you blind?"

I wave a hand right in front of his eyes as if to verify whether he can really see. My attempt to lighten things up a little has the opposite effect on him. I have clearly unnerved him. Mental note to self. Nix on the humor. We are not amused.

Waterman drops his eyes back down to his glass and studies the lone ice cube intently. I let him. I take a moment to recover the right air.

"I get it that you were trying to be nice," I offer. "Yah, I still have the long hair, even if it's gone all gray now."

"Yeah, that's what I meant. Your hair, you know, the way you look." He seems ready to get up and bolt out. I know this even before he says, "Maybe this wasn't such a good idea after all."

"Relax, Ed." I take a slow slip from my Jack, the way he started to work his drink. "Why don't you just tell me in your own words what we're doing here?"

I have always found the phrase "in your own words" to be redundant. Who else's words are they going to be? But the phrase always seems to help affirm a necessary locus of control for potential clients whose lives have just taken a crazy and unexpected turn south.

He looks back up at me, takes a deep breath and drains the rest of his scotch in one gulp. I catch Marge's eye and tilt my head and she prepares another round. He looks in my direction, not really at me, and then takes another deep breath and says, "I need your help."

He kind of coughs the request out like one of my cats raising a hairball. They have to be tough words for the former Fr. Waterman to choke out to a bad actor like me. Marge sets two more drinks on the table then wanders back to the far end of the bar. I take a slow slip from my fresh drink to encourage him to treat his in the same way. Instead he takes another big gulp, but still just sits there not saying anything. I sit quietly and watch him. Cashmere overcoat, Brooks Brothers suit, button-collar Pima cotton shirt, and hand-woven silk paisley tie. Everything hangs on him comfortably, as well-tailored clothes will do, and looks like just what he is meant to be wearing, not like he is dressed up. He's the kind of guy who always appears to be about to convene a board meeting. Sitting here in a back table at St. Martin's he blends in about like the queen in a cat house. I decide that I need to get him talking again, about anything.

"How's the furniture business?"

He clears his throat and takes a more careful sip.

"That's one of the reasons why I am here," is all he says. He goes silent again. The glazed look in his eyes confuses me. It is like he has slipped miles away from me. He looks down at his drink and swirls the ice cube in what little whisky is left. I look at Marge and nod at Ed. She understands my sign and brings him another, which he takes from her distractedly before she can set it down on the coaster. I decide to nurse the Jack in my hand and not get any fuzzier than I have already become.

Business isn't getting the ball rolling, maybe family. "How's the wife?"

"Still dead," he says, bitterly, accusingly, as if I should have known. "Very suddenly six years ago."

"I'm sorry. Any kids?"

He shakes his head.

"I kind of fell apart when Clarice died. I guess I lost the will to go on. I decided to cash out of the business not long after her death. Fourteen stores. Did pretty well. There's just the trust now. I still manage that. We help fund three inner city parochial schools. Help out with parks and gardens. Clarice loved to garden..."

This is getting me nowhere. In a minute I'll be hearing how to cultivate bougainvillea in a Midwest climate. I am still clueless about why he wants to talk to me.

"Yah, right. But you and me now, we're here because..."

"You're a private investigator, right?"

I answer him with a nod and a tip of my glass in what I think is my best Mickey Spillane imitation.

"Private. Like confidential?"

"Says it right on my business card."

He nods.

"And are you still a Catholic? I mean, have you followed what's going on in the church? And are there people in the chancery whom you know you can trust?"

Ex-priests often seem to know more about what's going on downtown than those still in the hallowed ranks. But then ex-seminarians like me never get in the loop in the first place.

"Catholic? Not like you mean. Following the church? Kinda. Chancery contacts? They don't call it the chancery anymore, Ed. It's the Pastoral Center. It's over at the old Quigley Seminary."

He nods. "I went there."

"Yah, me too. Before I went to Mundelein. You remember Mundelein?"

Too long a visit with Jack has loosened my tongue and I wor-

14

ry for a moment that my last comment might antagonize Ed. Instead, or maybe it's just that his third drink is kicking in, he finally seems to relax.

"Yeah, sorry about that, I guess. Water under the bridge, huh? It's all worked out for the better, though, hasn't it?"

He gives out a nervous little laugh.

"Is that really what it looks like to you?" I put my drink down. No more for me. I know that I better start controlling what I am saying. Brain first, Cosmo, then tongue. I take a second to stretch myself over the sore spot. "Okay, Ed. Let's you and me let the past be the past. Neither of us can change it. Why don't you just tell me what the hell you want."

"I want to hire you to investigate a murder."

"Clarice?"

"Oh, good grief, no. She had a stroke."

"Whose then?"

He jabs a thumb at his chest. "Mine."

He reaches into his jacket pocket and pulls out an unmarked envelope and lays it on the table between us.

"That's five thousand in cash. If you agree to what I ask now it's yours free and clear. If nothing happens to me, you'll never hear from me again. It'll be the easiest five grand you ever earned."

He sits back and finishes the last of his drink in one gulp. Before I can half give Marge another signal, he shakes his head.

"I have to drive downtown to meet someone tonight and I can't drink like I used to."

"What makes you think you're in danger? Who would want to murder you? And what the hell does the church have to do with it?"

He raises a hand as if to block my questions.

"Maybe I'm just being paranoid. I don't want to embarrass myself. And most especially don't want to cause the church any unwarranted embarrassment. But if anything happens to me beyond what usually happens to a man my age, and I don't care if it's...it's..." He hesitates and then continues, "...if it's tomorrow or if it's ten years from now, I expect you to check it out thoroughly."

He stops talking but doesn't look away from me.

"You don't want to give me a clue about what you suspect? Who you suspect? I don't get it. What am I supposed to investigate?"

He finally looks away, over my shoulder, like he is peering back at the past, or maybe into the future.

"Don't worry," he says, "You'll know. You'll receive a message. Maybe from the grave. And trust me, you will know what to do with it when you get it. If you expose the person or persons responsible for my death, I have made provisions for my foundation to cut you a cashier's check for two hundred thousand dollars. I'm afraid you will have to just trust me on that. We won't be signing any contract." He pushes the envelope on the table towards me. "One more thing. We never had this conversation. If you tell anyone about it, the deal is off. I know you will be checking up on me. I can't stop you. I don't even mind. Just do it with discretion. I am hoping and praying the foundation won't require the services you are agreeing to."

Ed Waterman reaches across the table to shake my hand. It is steady now. I take it with a firm grip. When he gets up to leave, I stand up with him. For a moment I think he is going to give me a hug. He doesn't. He just turns without another word and walks out of the bar. I throw some bills on the table, stuff the envelope into my pocket and follow him out the door. I watch him put his head down into the wind as he walks to a black Audi R8 parked half a block up the street. A blast of the frigid air that had followed him into the bar chafes my face as I stand alone in the open doorway. A winter storm is brewing.

CHAPTER THREE

The wind rattling at my window woke me way too early the next morning. I wanted to go back to sleep but my two cats whined to be fed and were all over my bed telling me to get the hell up. My mouth was dry and my bladder full. I felt like I might have swallowed my pillow during the night. I lay there still in my underwear blaming it on the sticky rice with mangoes at the Indie Café. No way the fifth of Jack I drank had anything to do with it. I cursed myself for forgetting to feed the cats from the bag of cat food I somehow remembered to pick up on my way home. And now they were giving me the business about it. As for my bladder, it seems that the frequency with which I need to empty it increases in direct proportion to the numbers of candles I blow out on my birthday cake. I looked at the watch still on my wrist and saw it was 9:30 already. I got up, ripped open the cat chow, fed the cats, and headed for the shower. Just as I stepped into the shower I heard my land line ring. I am not sure why I even have one. No one ever calls me at home. It would have to wait.

The shower felt good, rinsing all that fuzziness down the drain. A year back I splurged on a rainforest showerhead and have never once regretted the expense. Standing under it I began to make a mental list of who I needed to talk to about Ed Waterman. First would be Don Bruster. He left the seminary not far behind me and, like so many other wannabes who never made it past half-baked, became a lawyer. He worked his way up to Corporation Counsel in the Harold Washington administration. While he'd fallen away from the priesthood he'd stuck with the church and was ordained a permanent deacon. Don was a big-time judge by the time he retired. Being both a deacon and a judge I suppose he could sign his name "The Honorable Reverend Donald Bruster." He mentioned his plans to retire from the bench at a big South Side communion breakfast a couple years back, and before his eggs got cold the cardinal drafted him to arbitrate the constant bickering among the transaction guys and the litigators in the diocesan law office. Don actually seemed to enjoy doing this pro bono work, and settled into an untitled position of de facto power and influence at the chancery. He might well have heard of something through the pipeline I needed to know about.

I also decided to call another former classmate, a cop named Tom Keystone. He and I spent a whole lot of time together in the basement meditation chapel at Niles College Seminary, where Tom figured out that the scent of burning incense covered the pungent aroma of all the pot we smoked.

We seminarians were invited to lunch with Cardinal Cody once, at his residence high on the Gold Coast, just south of Lincoln Park. We dined on shrimp etouffée and beef bourguignonne served on Wedgewood china lighter than hummingbird wing. The crystal water glasses sung if you wiped a wet finger across their rim, and the art on the walls around us rivaled that in the museum ten minutes south. We were dismissed after a brief pep talk from the cardinal, something about virtue, as I remember. Probably humility too. As we were walking down the steps to the bus awaiting us on North State Parkway, Tom turned to me and said, "Oh, man, if this is poverty, bring on the chastity!"

The end of sophomore year he met a girl, fell in love, left the seminary, and became a Chicago cop. He married the girl and moved to the Southwest Side of the city where she grew up, one of those neighborhoods filled with cops and firemen. He turned out to be a pretty good cop. I see his name in the paper a couple times a year, usually a high profile case. Once or twice he's even shown up on the local news being interviewed by some blonde Barbie about one of Cook County's more entertaining homicides. He was, in fact, the guy who talked me into applying for my P.I. license. He was looking at maybe another year or two before retirement. We get together now and again over a glass or two and tell each other lies. I tried to remember how long it had been, and could not name the date. Tom is the closest thing to a friend that I have.

I stepped out into the February cold, walking around the block, hitting the alarm button on my key until I finally found my car. My hair was still wet from the shower and was wickedly cold and started to frost over by the time I found the car. I never wear a hat. It just doesn't feel right with the long hair.

I took my usual route down Clark Street, listening to ominous reports of impending lake-effect snow. I decided to park in the Century Mall lot to avoid getting towed when the snow started. Clark and Diversey are both snow routes. Two inches or more and they start impounding anything parked there. Better eight dollars parking than a couple hundred for a ticket and a tow.

I hate walking through the mall. All the empty stores depress me. I remember when I was growing up going to see double features with cartoons there on Saturday mornings. There was nothing left of the old movie palace but its forlorn marquee, with the name of the last movie that ever played there still plastered on it in big block letters. The mall has never been embraced by the neighborhood and can be as quiet as a graveyard at midmorning, with sales posters lined up mute as tombstones along the empty concourses. At least the shop where I buy my rolling papers is still open. I stepped out to the street and headed south past my office to grab a bite at Frances' Deli. Spoiled by success in my view, it hasn't been the same since they fired all the old

Jewish waitresses and moved down the street to where the yuppies could find them. But I knew that the huge omelets there still covered a lot of acreage and that the coffee would be strong and plentiful.

The walk back down the winter street to my office afterwards was less than pleasant. The wind whipping off the lake was growing stronger and stinging my face. My eyes were weeping from it just a few steps outside the deli. The clouds were turning dark gray and looked heavy enough to bring the Second City to a standstill if they ever opened up. I was grateful for the hissing of the steam radiator in the lobby when I finally reached the shelter of my building.

I always feel good when I open the door to my second-floor office. It is my space, not something I inherited. The private cave of Cosmo Grande. It has my stamp on it. It smells like me and it's rumpled and unkempt like me. There's a dorm-room fridge with a couple trays of ice cubes and usually a carton of half-eaten kung pao something or other. The client chair is usually piled with old sports sections and a dozen unread paperbacks, and there's a bottle of Jack in the top drawer of the filing cabinet, filed under T for "Tennessee whiskey," kept there in the event of unforeseen emergencies.

I hung my coat on the hook on the closet door. Like the radiator in the lobby, the one behind my desk was hotter than a baked potato and gave out a satisfying clatter. No worry about getting cold in here. I settled into the old wooden desk chair and phoned The Honorable Reverend Donald Bruster at the Pastoral Center. I went right into his voice mail and left a message to call me on my cell phone as soon as he could. As I hung up I patted my pocket and realized that I had left my cell phone at home again. Before I had a chance to look up Tom Keystone's number at the 1st District, the phone rang. It was Tom calling me. How convenient.

"You saved me a quarter. I was just about to call you," I laughed.

He was not in a joking mood. "Why the hell don't you answer any of your phones? I've been leaving you messages everywhere."

I only noticed then the message light blinking on my old Ma Bell phone.

"You're talking to me now, aren't you?"

"Stay at your office. Me and my new partner have official business with you."

"If it's about me using your name to get the Denver boot off my car..."

"Just sit tight and be ready to tell me all you know about your old buddy Ed Waterman."

"Waterman? That's really strange. I was—"

"Don't say another word, Mr. Grande. We're just getting off the drive at Belmont and we'll be there in ten minutes max. Be ready to tell us why a guy like Waterman had your business card."

"Mr. Grande" was a pretty clear warning. Tom was feeding me more than he had to. I figured he didn't completely trust his new partner. But I decided to push for a little more anyway. "Why don't you ask Waterman?"

"Ed Waterman is dead. He was found in his apartment on Monroe Street early this morning. Maybe a suicide, but I'm wondering whether he might have been murdered."

Does it make me a bad person that the first thing to cross my mind was the $200,000 paycheck he promised me if I'd investigate anything that happened to him? I've had worse thoughts. I kept this one to myself.

"I thought he lived in Wilmette," was all I could think to say.

"The mansion out there is still in his name. But he hasn't spent much time there since his wife died. They kept a place downtown where they could land after an evening of being seen at those charity functions they went to. They'd spend the night in

21

the city and then drive home to Wilmette in the morning."

"How did he die?"

"Since I'm the cop and you're the suspect, how about if I make up the questions and you make up the answers? Six minutes," he said, and hung up.

I cleared some fast food wrappers off the desk and rinsed a couple dead coffee cups in the bathroom sink until Tom and his partner walked into my office five minutes later without me buzzing them in. Keystone carried himself like a guy who was counting the days before he could retire. He was a big unmade bed of a man even in his salad days, and was looking more rumpled than usual now. Dispeptic. Grumpy. Not a man to suffer fools gladly. His partner, on the other hand, looked about as world-weary as a cocker spaniel puppy. He was wearing an off-the-rack J.C. Penney suit with a standard drop and was clean shaven and wearing an expression that made you want to call him "kid" and send him out for fresh donuts.

"Take notes, kid. My arthritis is killing me," Tom said, as if on cue.

He slumped down on the edge of my desk and stared straight at me for a moment without speaking, as if warning me not to put on the smart-ass show for the kid we both knew I was capable of.

"So what was my vic doing with your business card in his wallet?"

"How should I know? I print 500 of them at a time and pass them out in cocktail lounges. What if I told you I haven't seen Waterman since the day he gave me the toss?"

The kid immediately looked up from his notepad. "The toss from where?" Motive. Wow. He was already thinking about his next promotion.

Tom answered for me. "The seminary. Mr. Grande and I were classmates. We used to..." He paused. "We used to medi-

22

tate together."

"Someone must have given him my card," I said. "I got a lot of them floating around out there. That's how come I can afford this sumptuous life style."

The kid snorted. Then I remembered a curious thing. I never did give Waterman my card.

"Forensics says it looks like a suicide, and downtown seems happy enough to close the books on it. Maybe they're right."

Tom's eyes were saying something different from his words. The kid was missing all of it, taking notes like there was going to be a quiz on Thursday.

"You think of anything or figure out how he got your card, you give me a call," Tom said. "We're on until three today."

He was telling me to sit tight and expect a call from him when his partner wasn't around.

The partner looked up from his pad and said aggressively, "FYI, you will remain an official person of interest until this case is settled."

"Easy, Andy. Cool your jets. I'm sure Mr. Grande understands that. He won't do anything stupid," he said with a lot of emphasis on the stupid, no doubt for my benefit. He stood up to leave. I shook his hand and reached for the kid's.

"Nice meeting you Andy. Andy...?"

"We'll be in touch," he said coolly, leaving my outstretched hand unshaken. He turned and followed Tom out the door with a final dismissive snort.

I sat back down in my chair and resisted the urge to bring the Old No. 7 out from the file cabinet. It wasn't even noon yet. And I had to think. It just couldn't be suicide, not so soon after Ed handed me the envelope still bulging in my coat pocket. Coincidences happen, sure, but believing in them never got me anywhere. All I could do was wait to hear what Tom actually had. But I was pretty certain that he wasn't about to tell me anything unless I spilled my guts, violating that one condition of secrecy that Ed gave me yesterday and jeopardizing my $200,000 payday. Yeah, that had crossed my mind. I had to figure out a strategy and I had to do it fast. I thought again about Don Bruster and wondered what he could tell me.

I didn't have to wait long. Don returned my call shortly after Tom left with his new puppy.

"Sorry I didn't get back to you sooner. It's been as crazy around here. The cardinal and Gallo have called in O'Halloran and Scarpetti, all the big guns in the law department, leaving me to catch flak."

I never acquired a taste for the intrigue that chanceries everywhere seem to breed, but I knew I ought to at least feign interest.

"What's going on? Why is the big guy's red cassock tied in a knot?"

"I can only tell you this much. A former priest, like way back former, you know, an old guy, I can't tell you his name, but a recent widower, a man who got stalled trying to get reinstated, you know. Full court press. Petitions to the cardinal. Phone calls to the nuncio. Appeals to the curia. Anyway, we just heard this morning that he committed suicide. In despair, they think, over the church's refusal to let him back in."

"Ed Waterman."

"How the hell could you know that? They got the lid so tight on this his family hasn't even been notified yet."

"Don, we have to talk, face-to-face, as soon as we can."

"You know Wing Ho on Sheridan Road?"

"Sure."

"At seven tonight. Until then, whatever else you do, stay the hell out of it and keep your trap shut."

24

CHAPTER FOUR

I had half an afternoon to find out all that I could about the late Ed Waterman. I Googled his name and all that came up were *Tribune* society pages and press accounts of his charitable work. He was wearing a tuxedo as comfortably as an old T-shirt in most of the pictures, usually with his pretty wife on his arm. She was one of those North Shore ladies who grow more handsome as they age, the kind that never sweat or break a fingernail. I came across her obituary and Ed's two brothers' death notices as well. I found one picture of him in his Knights of Malta regalia looking like he just stepped out of a crowd scene at a Lyric Opera matinee production of *Rigoletto*. A short recent article in the *National Catholic Reporter* detailed his request to reenter the active priesthood after his wife's death and its surprising rejection by Rome. Further back were a lot of stories about the purchase of Chicago's iconic furniture and appliance chain. Almost everybody in Chicago who isn't living in a cardboard box has bought something from Waterman's at some point in their lives.

The Waterman Foundation had a pretty good website and a ton of marshmallow prose about its generosity to inner city Catholic schools. The chain of stores had been privately held, so offered no public accounting of assets, but the financial statements of the foundation, a 501(c)(3) organization, were public, and they proved that the Waterman family had made boatloads of money selling chintzy furniture and low-end appliances on lay away. Between the money Ed made spinning off the business and his wife's inheritance, the foundation had very deep pockets. Ed Waterman was the Last of the Mohicans, so with every one of the major players dead the foundation's future could get very interesting. But there was nothing in what I found to help me understand why Waterman had reached out. I was just about to shut down the computer when Tom called.

"I'm emailing you the crime lab photos from a hidden IP address. Print hard copies for yourself, delete them from your computer, and do a government wipe of your drive when you're done. I don't want any Cook County prosecutors figuring out later how you got them."

"Dropped over the transom in the middle of the night by person or persons unknown."

"Take a look at them before we get together. I don't want to risk being seen back at your office. Meet me at Gulliver's on Howard."

"Why all the secrecy?"

"There's movement in the bush, baby. And this old dog's too close to retirement to get bushwhacked.

"Aren't you being paranoid?"

"Like they say, that don't mean they're not out to get me. One hour," he said, and hung up.

Tom sent sixty-eight images of Waterman's apartment. I printed them out and deleted them as asked. Deleting files does not remove them from your hard drive. It just takes down the sign posts pointing to them. Any modestly capable IT guy can dig them back up in a couple minutes. I used a disk-wiping utility a client had turned me onto and wrote multiple passes of 1's and 0's over my unused disk space. While the utility cleaned up the evidence of Keystone's collusion from the hard drive, I studied the sixty-eight shots. Nothing struck me as unusual. It appeared that Ed washed down a handful of Valium with his friend Johnny. The empty prescription bottle and a half-empty bottle of scotch sat on the bedside stand. He lay stretched across the middle of the bed with his arms splayed. He was still wearing the suit he had on when we met. He hadn't so much as loosened his tie. If there was anything you might call evidence in these photos it was hiding in plain sight.

I walked to my car in the Century lot. It still hadn't started to snow, but dark clouds scudded over the city like swords of heavenly retribution. It was on its way. I got on Lake Shore Drive at Belmont and drove north to perpetually congested Sheridan Road, past Loyola University's campus to Howard Street, the northern boundary of the city. I took it west to Gulliver's, where you could always find a quiet corner to meet someone without attracting attention.

I asked for Tom when I got there and the manager led me to a back table where Tom was sitting with a glass of ice and a can of diet Coke. He looked past me as I approached across the room as if to see if anyone had followed me in.

"A little privacy, Lou?" he said to the manager.

"No problem, Tom. I can keep this section empty until four at least." He turned to me, "Your pleasure?"

"I'll have what he's having," I said.

"So tell me what you found in the pictures," Tom said, all business. Something or someone had gotten under his skin.

"Looked a lot to me like a rich old guy who missed his dead wife. What did you see?"

"The same thing. A perfect story. A kid out of the academy could put it together in ten minutes. And that's what bothers me. But did you notice his tie?"

"He was always a tight ass, formal and stiff. Now he's just stiff."

"Yeah, but who doesn't loosen his tie when he walks into his house after a long day? You empty your pockets, you loosen your collar, maybe you kick off your shoes. These things are habitual.

Who stays buttoned down to commit suicide?"

"That's pretty thin, Tom. Your shorts aren't all twisted over a tight collar, are they? Why are we meeting here? What aren't you telling me?"

He glanced around the empty restaurant, almost unconsciously, like he was confirming no one was listening in.

"I got invited into this case by the commander himself. He picked me special, six weeks from retirement, out of rotation. It just don't happen that way. And then he pairs me up with a new rookie partner who don't know sugar beets from Shinola. *You* tell *me* why."

"So it never really gets investigated."

He nodded. "There's just this one little hitch."

"My business card."

He nodded. "Now's the part where you tell me everything, Cosmo. Every. Thing." he said, jabbing a finger at me twice for emphasis.

I thought a moment about that $200,000 pot of gold at the end of the Waterman rainbow, and how telling Tom the truth could jeopardize it. I figured, though, that I had a better chance of getting to it if I had an inside line on the police investigation, and Tom was never a guy to kiss and tell. I decided to take a leap of faith.

"I saw him yesterday. He gave me a retainer. Asked me to investigate if anything happened to him."

"Damn it! I knew it! I just knew it!" Tom was more than upset. He was apoplectic.

"He was very mysterious about it though. Said maybe he was only being paranoid, and I think he didn't want anyone going into a snit about him talking to me. He insisted that I not tell anybody about our arrangement, which I hope we can keep between us. It's kind of a condition of my employment. I was to sit on my hands unless something happened. He said something like he'd send a message from the grave, and that I'd know it when I saw it. Promised a pretty nice bump if I find anything."

"And the message?"

"I haven't heard a peep out of Ed Waterman's ghost all day."

Tom pulled out his cell phone and dialed. "Listen, kid," he said into the phone, "tell forensics to keep the Waterman scene secured."

I could just hear enough of Andy's reply to know he was objecting.

"I don't give a damn what the manager of the building says," Tom told him. "Keep the doors locked and the tape across them. I'm going to check it out again in the morning." He rolled his eyes at the kid's reply. "Yah, Andy, I know it's your day off. Christ, it's mine too. But you can just take it off. I'm only going to be there for a little bit. No need for you to be there." He listened for a moment. "I got new information from a C.I.," he said, and after a brief pause, "You know I can't tell you that. That's why we call them confidential. It's what the C stands for. Don't worry about me. Don't worry, I'll fill you in." He ended the call. "Soon as hell freezes over," he said to the dead phone.

Keystone shook the ice in his glass and looked back at me smiling ever so slightly. "Perfect. No one will be around if we get there early. And my new partner will still be fast asleep. So be there at seven, Cosmo. Let's see what your fresh pair of private eyes can come up with."

He stood up abruptly and walked towards the door and out into the cold, sticking me with the check, one of Tom's signature moves.

I decided to go home and pick up my cell phone before meeting Don in Edgewater. When I got there the cats curled at my legs, wanting to be fed again. I checked both my cell phone and the land line and found nothing more than voice mails from Tom trying to reach me earlier in the day. No chilling messages from the grave.

I took advantage of the time I had, and the fact that I'd been drinking cokes instead of whiskeys, to run through some Tae Kwon Do forms. I usually do them early in the morning, to keep my afternoons and evenings open for my buddy Jack, but if I go more than a day or two without a workout my body starts to cry out for it. My teacher was an inscrutable Korean immigrant named Sim. Whether that was his Christian name or his surname escaped even my vast powers of detection. He taught, in his broken English, that Tae Kwon Do was not just a martial art but a way of life. If you practice the discipline correctly, you are a coiled spring walking. "Readiness is all," he would tell us. Struggling with his R's, it sounded like "Weadiness is all." We, his students, would sometimes repeat it to one another, always well out of his hearing. "Weadiness is all." But we never forgot Sim's preaching about readiness and speed, and it has always stood me in good stead. In a street fight, about the time you have perfected your back stance and properly chambered your fist, the other guy is kicking you in the jewels. So I practice the discipline on an almost daily basis, trying to keep that edge honed and ready. The *K'ihaps* scare the heck out of the cats, and sometimes the upstairs neighbors, who wonder what all the shouting is about, but the forms really do strengthen my body and concentrate my mind. After forty minutes I was warm and lithe and soaked in sweat and my rectus abdominus was tauter than a brand new banjo string.

It was getting late, and I know Don Bruster doesn't suffer tardiness, so I jumped in the shower and changed. I stuffed my cell phone in my pocket and realized that I was still carrying Waterman's envelope of cash. I grabbed four hundred dollars and stashed the rest behind a book on a bottom shelf.

Don pulled into the restaurant parking lot at the same time I did. I could tell, even though he was wrapped up in a parka, that he had gained a lot of weight since leaving the bench. When you work for the church, putting on the pounds is an occupational hazard. You get invited to way too many banquets serving chicken cordon bleu. He greeted me with a firm handshake, which he held a little longer than I found comfortable. I never knew Don to do a day of physical labor in his life, but his ebony hand was hard as a pig's foot, and he pressed my limp fingers now to just below the threshold of pain. That part of the old Chicago politician in him had not retired. His ascent to the court as one of the few African-American judges was old-style Chicago politics start to finish, and the artifacts of that experience remained clearly at work. As soon as we walked into the restaurant we were escorted wordlessly to the empty banquet hall upstairs. The hostess turned on some lights, sat us in a corner, bowed ever so slightly to Don, and left us. I felt like Humphrey Bogart might come strolling through the door any minute with a smoke between his fingers and a pained expression crossing his brow. The hostess brought out an unordered Jack on the rocks for me and a glass of ice water for Don. She left as silently as she had arrived.

"Listen, Cosmo, anything we say is strictly off the record. Consider it a heads-up from a good friend. The boss wants some answers from you."

I took a gulp of the drink. "You forget, I work for myself, Don. I don't have a boss and I like it that way."

"I'm talking about my boss, the cardinal."

"He may be your boss, but he isn't mine. The late Ed Waterman made sure of that. But I never did kowtow to cardinals. This'd be a damn funny time to start."

"Well, you'll be happy to know that he won't be the one asking the questions. It'll be his hatchet man, Gallo."

Billy Gallo was the unlikely chancellor of the archdiocese. He rose from being a parish business manager in Cicero to becoming the most powerful lay Catholic in Chicago. He got there by putting his arms around the right shoulders at the right time and, some say, by putting his hands in the right pockets. It was well-understood that he had connections at city hall and whispered that he was more than familiar with what is left of the Chicago syndicate. But then again, any powerful Italian American in this city risks being tarred with that rumor. I have had heard it flung at me more than once, usually answered with a well-placed kick to a soft spot on the flinger's body.

Bruster was a Knight of Malta, like Waterman and probably Gallo, and a former CYO light heavyweight boxing champion who still relished sparring verbally with anyone who dared challenge him.

"And what, Honorable Deacon Don, might those questions be about?"

"Stop playing dumb, Cosmo. People are starting to believe you really are. Everyone downtown is buzzing about Waterman's alleged suicide, and it's in risk of getting all gummed up in internal politics. We can use your help."

He was quiet while a waiter rolled out a tray of dim sum and arrayed baskets of food and bowls of sauce across the tablecloth. I had expected Don to tell me to keep my head down and try to stay out of it. The church, especially in Chicago, has a history of trying to fix its own problems, and Don is one of the key guys they turn to when it's time to pour oil on troubled waters. I was surprised by the frankness of his opening gambit.

He unwrapped a pair of chopsticks, rolled them between his hands, and then stabbed at a dumpling, dipped it in a bowl of broth, and popped it into his mouth. When the waiter withdrew he said, "You've got to tell Billy Gallo everything you know, Cosmo. Please. Even what you just suspect. I don't give a flying fig what your feelings are about Waterman or the cardinal or the church or the pope in Rome. I just need you to trust me on this one even if it starts to go sideways. Especially if it starts to go sideways. If what I'm afraid is true really is true, Billy is the only guy I know who has any hope of reeling it in."

I picked at a spare rib. Don reached for his napkin and started dabbing at a spot on his tie.

"Now, you know Billy. He'll try to piss you off. That's part of his act. He'll want you off-balance. Off your game. I promise I'll be watching your back with all the resources I have at my disposal. And I have more than you probably think." He folded the napkin and wiped his brow. The room wasn't that warm, but he had worked himself into a sweat.

I piled a little hot mustard and duck sauce on a crab rangoon, trying to find that elusive perfect balance of heat and sweet. That wasn't the toughest conundrum I was facing. I didn't know what the hell to make of what I'd just heard. Guys like Don usually stick to a simple strategy of deny, deny, deny. Put your head down and dig. What people don't know won't hurt them. But here he was going the opposite way. Bringing me on board. Making me a member of the team.

This case was born in the dark, and I was still floundering in the dark, but if I was sure of nothing else in this life, I was sure of one thing: I wasn't about to tell him or Gallo one damn thing. It was almost like I didn't want to tell them just because they wanted so badly to know. I needed to put a battle plan together before I decided to share with the group. I needed to buy a little time. Don was looking for cooperation. I folded a little moo shu pork into a pancake with a dollop of hoisin and took a contemplative bite, like I was weighing all he'd said.

"If Billy Gallo calls me, I'll go see him," I said. "I'll be as forthcoming as I am able to be. I am not promising I can shed any light."

Don closed his eyes briefly and when he reopened them said in scarcely more than a whisper. "I know that I am leaving you with a lot of unanswered questions. But please trust me on this.

And don't tell anyone, anyone, that we had this conversation. Do you understand?"

"Got it," I said, touching a finger to the side of my nose. I decided not to wink.

"The bill is paid. Wait five minutes after I leave before going downstairs."

He reached his hand across the table. This time the handshake was a little less firm, but a whole lot warmer.

The snowflakes still had not started to fly when I hit the street a few minutes later. After an uneventful drive home I slipped the key into the lock to my front door and it turned without resistance. The door, which I was sure I had locked carefully when I left, was not locked now. My Rock Island Armory 206 .38 caliber double-action revolver with a cross-hatched Walnut grip and a two-inch barrel for easy concealment was sitting under a pile of not-so-tighty whiteys thirty feet beyond the door that someone other than me had opened within the last two hours.

CHAPTER FIVE

I figured if someone was in the condo, he or she might be pointing my own gun at the door right now. I stood to the side, turned the knob slowly, and swung the unlocked door open. Every light in the house was on. Despite the door and the lights, I started to relax. The cats suggested no assassins lurked in waiting. Cleo was lying on top of my old Zenith TV, her favorite place, and Zimmerman was rubbing up against the coffee table and purring. If somebody was in the condo, those two would be cowering under the bed. I shouted out a loud hello just to be sure, and was answered only by silence.

I walked into the bedroom to check the dresser first. I grabbed the gun and checked that the next cylinder was hot in the unlikely event that the cats proved wrong. Waterman's cash was where I'd left it. I tiptoed through the rest of the apartment. Nothing seemed to be missing. The crime scene photos were still at the office. There was nothing on the coffee table but some unpaid bills.

Still, some things were not right. The screen on my computer was flickering. I always turn it off before I go out. I booted it and opened up my email to check my messages. Everything sensitive was password protected, so I doubted I'd been breached in any meaningful way. I typed in "jacksfriend" and the screen went bright blue and big white letters started spelling out DONTGOTHERE!DONTGOTHERE! over and over again as if some blue-screen-of-death virus had taken over the computer. But once the letters had filled the screen, it all disappeared and I found myself looking at my regular desktop background.

I went into the kitchen, where the ceiling light was still on, just as I had left it. But tossed into the sink were a dozen cans of beer from my refrigerator, open and inverted with all the beer gone down the drain. Worse than that, the handle of Jack Daniels that I keep in the cabinet over the stove for days like this was neck down in the sink, empty as well. I headed back into the bathroom. A small, stuffed animal, a kitten, was hanging from a noose wrapped over the showerhead. Somebody was doing a pathetic job of trying to scare me and a heroically great job of pissing me off. I tore down the dangling cat toy. Beyond that, the only thing that I could find that had been touched was my old Jerusalem Bible, the one I studied back in the seminary. It had been taken from the bookcase where I kept it and left splayed open on the tattered old footstool in my living room. I picked it up, closed it, and put it back up on the dusty shelf. I started back to the kitchen for a quick nerve medicine before remembering the jug of whiskey inverted in my sink. I turned in disgust and went and sat down on the couch in front of the television.

I was mostly concerned that there was no sign of forced entry. I throw the deadbolt religiously, so it's not like some amateur slipped the latch with a credit card. Someone either got his hands on a key or knew an awful lot about how to pop a good lock. Not like it was neighborhood kids. A pro. I got up and dead-bolted and chained the door in case whoever it was decided to come back again in the middle of the night. I collapsed into my favorite chair and flipped the television on. When the picture appeared I found it was tuned into EWTN, an ultra-conservative Catholic cable network I never watch. It was founded by a nun who looked and sounded like every Catholic grammar school child's worst nightmare. On the screen, in living color, assuming an air of forced humility, was the Right Reverend Bishop Michael Mc-Tighue of Tulsa, Oklahoma, the very seminary dean Waterman had reported me to way back when. McTighue was the man who officially gave me my walking papers.

As far as I could tell, the purpose of his oratory was to straighten everyone out about the paramount importance of putting the tabernacle holding the hosts in the correct place on the altar. I guess he thought God Almighty has decorating standards like anyone else. He used a lot of broad gestures, more like a man on stage than an actor in front of a television camera, tugging at his cape and waving his hands in front of him to make sure that the audience got a good look at his jewel-studded episcopal ring. I remembered why I always skip through this station.

Then the question hit me. How did EWTN, which I would not turn to if Satan himself was tormenting me, end up as my last-watched channel? Was it a coincidence that Waterman and McTighue reappeared in my life, simultaneously, after all those years? Since I was out of Jack and the beer was gone, I briefly debated the opposing sides of my present dilemma: stay straight or get high. Getting high made by far the better argument, so I went into the kitchen and picked a couple roaches out of an ashtray and rolled a fresh joint from what dregs I found there. I bent over the gas burner on the stove to fire it up and went back to the television hoping to take the edge off a rough day. After a few deep tokes I swear that the bishop morphed into Sean Hannity and railed at me about my errant ways. I drifted into asleep.

━━━

Linda Ronstadt, wearing one of those crumpled cowboy hats, stopped singing "Blue Bayou" right in my ear. She got off my lap and reached for the clamoring phone. When I woke up, I was sprawled on my couch. It was light outside and two old priests were confabulating about the body of Christ on the television and my land line was ringing to beat hell. My mouth was dry and I was still half in my dream. Why didn't Linda answer the damn phone? Did she have violet eyes? Where did she disappear to? I reached for the phone and pulled it to my ear, and growled "Yeah."

Tom Keystone's angry voice brought me fully awake.

"Where the hell are you?"

I looked at my watch. 7:15. "I'm out the door right now. I'll see you in fifteen minutes."

My condo, which I inherited from my brother, along with Cleopatra the cat, was on Fremont in Wrigleyville. Primo always liked being in the neighborhood around Dad's grocery store, even after their epic falling out. I like that it is so close to Lake Shore Drive and even more that it was paid for before my brother died. That all happened before the neighborhood became young, and trendy, and desirable, and occasionally insufferable to an old North Side dog like yours truly. It's worth a lot more now than what Primo paid for it. The only real downside is that parking is impossible, especially during baseball season. I have this habit of tossing parking tickets, and get the Denver boot often enough that I wish they'd change the color to something that coordinates better with my car's interior. Still, I plan on sticking around if the yuppies and the taxmen don't chase me away.

I splashed some water on my face and headed out the door. I had no time to change the clothes that I had slept in. I did remember my cell phone, though I had neglected to charge it overnight. Yesterday's threat of snow had become today's reality. I sloshed through three wet inches of it to reach my car a block away. The snow was still falling heavily and nobody was bothering to shovel yet. I swiped the windshields clean with my bare hands. Pretty soon I was going to have to start getting ready for winter. When I finally sat in the car I put my numb fingers under my coat into my armpits to warm them up. I turned the radio to WBBM Newsradio for a traffic and weather report. Lake Shore

Drive was bumper-to-bumper to Navy Pier, and the Kennedy Expressway was crawling to the Loop. No surprise. Lake effect snows usually snarled everything.

I decided to cut over to Halsted, along with about a thousand other frustrated drivers. I called a local locksmith as I inched along and left a message about rekeying the lock on my front door.

Chicago is still a city of neighborhoods, even if the folks living in them have changed over the years. We Chicagoans mainly live our lives out in our select slice of the pie. The drive through Boystown with its gay bars, past Greektown and its tourist-ridden flaming cheese restaurants, would normally have taken twenty-five minutes, but was double that today because of the weather. When I finally parked in a city lot across from the Presidential Towers, I knew it had to be past 8:30 without looking at my watch. I stopped and picked up two large black coffees from the coffee shop next door as a peace offering to Tom who, I knew, would be heroically ticked. The doorman found my name on his clipboard and waved me up to Waterman's twenty-third floor apartment. I expected a uniformed cop to be guarding the entrance. There wasn't one. The door was closed but unlocked and the yellow tape I expected to find was nowhere to be seen. So I walked right into a setting that screamed of the soulless hauteur of East Coast interior design. Not rooms to be lived in, but to be showcased and envied. Not the comforts of home, a place to eat your deep dish pizza out of the box while the Cubs blew another one, but decorated with the hard-purchased, discriminating taste that nobody with warm blood and a beating heart ever really liked. Everything was top-of-the-line, from the burnished mahogany floors to the sparkling Murano glass chandeliers. The taupe draperies, pinch-pleated and tailored to fit floor to ceiling, were drawn open. What would have been a stunning view of the downtown skyline was obstructed by the waves of white snow falling harder now than during my drive.

I figured Tom must be in the bedroom. Before I had a chance to announce my presence I felt the cell phone vibrate in my pocket. I set the two coffees on the shining top of an antique clawfoot Victorian table just past the foyer, the first time in that piece of furniture's life, I was sure, that hot coffee got anywhere near its lacquered top. I didn't much care if I left a couple rings behind. I stepped into the hallway to take the call. It was the locksmith telling me that he would be able to get to my condo that afternoon, sometime around three, depending on how bad the storm got.

When I walked back in, Tom was standing in the foyer waiting for me. He picked up one of the coffees like he'd just been waiting for me to deliver it, took a sip, looked right past me, and said, "You look like you slept in those clothes and you smell like Willie Nelson's cat."

"Never were no flies on you," I said. "I had a little bit of a night. So what do you want me to see now that I'm here?"

He turned and led the way into the bedroom. We passed a bathroom marbled on all six faces and no larger than the lobby at Orchestra Hall. It was spotless. The 700-gram Egyptian cotton bath towels looked like they had never been touched by human hands. The bedroom was sumptuous, everything about it bigger than life: oversized, overstuffed, overdesigned, and overpriced. Waterman's body had already been taken to the morgue. There were no apparent signs of struggle. No misplaced furnishings or torn draperies, no drag marks on the good Berber carpet. On the bed a blue silk comforter had been turned down as if someone planned on getting into bed in the next few minutes. The sheets were crisp and shiny and I'm sure had a high-three-digit thread count, but they clearly had not been slept on. The only sign that something may have gone amiss here was the carbon-black fingerprint powder dusted on most hard surfaces in the room.

Tom must have read my mind. "The powder is my doing. I got some pretty clear prints and I have a friend who'll run them for me without a paper trail. Old open case number, so no trail."

The empty pill bottle, the half-spent bottle of scotch, and a glass tumbler sat just where you'd expect them to be, arranged on a nightstand next to the bed, just where Waterman might have left them.

"Looks square to me," I said. "Except for there being no note. Wasn't Waterman the kind of guy who would want to get the last word in?"

"It stinks," he said, without offering one iota of evidence why. Keystone has always been one of those guys who act out of their guts.

"It's either exactly what it's supposed to be or a very sharp piece of funny business. You sure you want to risk your pension on it?"

Before he could answer, my phone vibrated again. Tom turned away, feigning no interest in the call, but I knew better. I ambled down the hall to the marble master bath, closed the door, and sat on the lidded toilet. Saying "Hello," my voice echoed like I was in a cathedral.

A woman's voice on the other end of the call identified herself as Kelley Morrissey.

"Mr. Grande, I am Mr. Gallo's secretary, calling from the Archdiocese of Chicago's Pastoral Center. Mr. Gallo needs to see you on a matter of utmost importance and would like to meet you at his office at three o'clock today. Can you confirm you can be here?"

I had the locksmith coming at three, and was anxious to secure the condo.

"Doesn't really work for me. How about some time tomorrow?"

"I'm sorry," she said. "I'm not making myself clear. I know

what I said sounded like a request, but it is more like a summons. Mr. Gallo instructed me not to allow you to underestimate the importance of his seeing you today. He was quite adamant that I needed to assure your cooperation."

"Okay, lady, three o'clock it is."

I crept to the door and opened it suddenly, figuring I might catch Tom standing nearby, trying to hear a bit of my conversation. But he wasn't there. When I walked back into the bedroom he was sitting in a wingback leather chair with his feet propped up on an antique footstool, reading from a very-expensive-looking leather-bound bible. He was sipping his coffee from his paper cup and reading from the large book propped on his lap. He didn't seem to notice I was back.

He looked up when I stood right over him.

"Funny, nobody said anything about this bible when they searched the room for evidence. It was sitting right here on the footstool not five feet from Waterman's body. And nobody thought to check it out."

"And?"

"We both know what a neat freak Waterman was. So the first thing I see when I open it up is the holy card from his wife's wake."

"People stick holy cards into their bibles all the time. I wouldn't get any big ideas about it."

"How's this for a big idea, Cosmo? You shut your pie hole and I get to make my point?"

I made a go-ahead gesture.

"It's such a beautiful bible. Got to be hand bound. Probably a Waterman family heirloom, worth a lot of money. But with one leaf torn out. So how could Ed bring himself to tear up a family heirloom? Or let someone else do it? And why did someone stick the Mass card right where the leaf was torn out?"

"Let me see."

Tom handed the bible over to me and drained the last of the coffee from his cup. The bible was beyond beautiful. It had clearly been more than an object d'art to Waterman. It wasn't something that he kept on a shelf and took down occasionally to admire. The supple leather cover was hand tooled and worn and actually stained from the oils on hands that obviously held it frequently. The gilt edge on the pages was tarnished almost to gray. The pages were not stiff and fresh from lack of use. Some sections, like Psalms, actually were beginning to look a little dog-eared from frequent turning. This was not a museum piece. It was a living spiritual discipline. I checked which page had been torn out and made a mental note of it. It was from Genesis, starting midway through Chapter 14.

"Why didn't you dust the cover for prints?"

"I did," he said.

I held the book up so the light outside glared off the cover and flipped it around and found nary arch, nor loop, nor whorl.

"Leather's not that tough to lift a print from," I said. "This cover's been wiped."

"Not just wiped, Cosmo. Scrubbed. Sanitized. Even Waterman's latents are gone. They could have lasted for years if it hadn't been wiped."

"Maybe the page that was pulled is significant. I'll check it out when I get home. I'll let you know if I find anything interesting. I doubt it has anything to do with Waterman's death."

I wasn't sure myself if I believed what I'd just said, but I had decided to play my hand close to the vest.

Tom kept sitting on the chair looking around the room. I sat on the side of the bed. Even for a neatnik like Waterman, everything appeared just a little too orderly. It wasn't just the bible that had been scrubbed. The whole place had been sanitized. The bathroom was spotless. Even the toilet paper on the roll was folded to a point and cascaded, the way hotel maids do.

"Is it plausible," I ask, "that he just gets home from meeting me, pours himself a tall glass of whisky, gets his pills out of the bathroom, sits down on the bed, and swallows everything in that bottle we found? Never even takes off his suit coat or loosens his tie? No pajamas laid out. No robe on a hook. So why was the comforter turned back on the far corner of the bed like it was? There was no reason for Waterman to do it."

"No marks on his body," Tom says, continuing my line of thinking. "No sign of forced entry. Everything in every room seemed to be exactly as it should be. Not so much as a mislaid newspaper or a pair of slippers not tucked away in the closet. It's too neat, even for Waterman."

We both stood up and looked around the room some more, as if that would make a clue jump up for our inspection. There was nothing. Tom tucked the bible under his arm and we stepped out and closed the door on the empty apartment.

Parking set me back thirty bucks. We hadn't been in the apartment for two hours. At least my car had been under a roof and I didn't have to clear off the snow that had fallen since I left it. Despite the six inches now on the street, I decided to drive back to my office to see if whoever hit my apartment had visited there too.

CHAPTER SIX

It was still snowing wicked hard, but the main streets were remarkably clear and echelons of salt trucks were working overtime. Former mayor Jane Byrne stole the mayor's office in 1979 when Daley's handpicked successor, incumbent Michael Bilandic, made the mistake of underestimating the toll a heavy blizzard would take just before election day. Traffic was snarled for days, with even major streets impassable. Marooned voters were stuck at home watching political ads on television. With snow cascading all around, Byrne promised an end to the Machine's incompetence. The media pundits were about evenly torn between calling her election a "snowslide" and an "avalanche." There never has been much creativity in Chicago's fourth estate. Since that frozen fiasco, quickly plowing winter streets has remained an absolute must for whoever wants to keep sitting in the mayor's office.

I spotted a small lot shoveled and open near my office but found myself leaning into a strong head wind the entire two blocks from there. I shook the snow from my shoulders in the lobby and found my office door locked, just the way I had left it. Despite its age, the old building was about as secure as you can expect, with an intercom and security buzzer to gain entry to the building and deadbolt locks on every door.

Next door to me on my right was the office of Levinson and Son. I never saw the son, just old Levinson, and for all I knew the son was a piece of fiction dreamed up for marketing purposes. He was a tailor of fine handmade suits who worked under a bare light bulb hanging from a cord, past midnight every night but Friday, with his door open and his head bowed at his work. He would always look up when I walked by, often with a great long pair of scissors in his hand, shake his head and mutter, "Boy, what a new suit and a haircut could do for your business, Mr. Grande."

On my left was Chang's Oriental Trader. There was no Chang as far as I could tell, just Sandy Cashman, a former lawyer who was disbarred in the 1970s for reasons time itself has forgotten. Now a purveyor of novelties, she is always in her office when I come in, no matter how early I arrive. If she sees me in the hallway or on the steps, she'll reach into her pocket and give me a telescoping back scratcher or a pen that plays "God Bless America" when you write with it or a wind-up flashlight that never needs batteries, all made by coolie labor in some dark hole in the Far East. I figured that my office was extra secure with the two of them around.

The safe in my closet was just as I had left it. I opened it and took out the crime scene photos from the attaché case, tore them up, stuffed them in a Walgreens bag and tossed it in the can at the end of the hallway. I still had a few hours before I had to venture back out into the snow and grant an audience to Chancellor Gallo. So I sat at my desk and grabbed the bottle from the file cabinet and poured a couple of fingers into an old Starbucks cup I kept in the drawer with it.

"Missed you last night, buddy," I said. I leaned back in my chair and chugged it down in one gulp. First one fast, indeed.

A single message was waiting on the office answering machine. It was Don, telling me to call him on his cell between noon and one o'clock so we could talk while he was out to lunch, far from the prying ears of the Pastoral Center. I looked at my watch. It was ten to one. I invited Jack back for another visit, promising myself to drink this one slower. I sipped it for five minutes and then gave Don a call.

ter Auditorium. The space had been transformed into an en-
nce no less grand than any of the five star hotels choking the
ghborhood. There was not a vestige of the old school left.

The receptionist sat at a great white travertine desk not larg-
han the quarter deck of the USS Constitution.

"Mr. Grande," she said as I walked through the door. Her
r was thin and frayed and died the color of an Afghan war-
d's henna beard. Her smile, while efficient and professional,
absent of any real warmth, just what the building felt like.
older gentleman with a plastic name tag that read "Mr. Mike
eigh" clipped a temporary tag with my name printed on it to
lapel and gestured toward the elevator.

"I'll walk you to Mr. Gallo's office. It's easier than trying to
you directions."

"I appreciate it." Security for the Center's sake, not mine, I
ught. I guess I do look like the type of guy who might pilfer a
ted plant. "Could I stop and have a peek at the stained glass in
chapel?" I asked. "I went to school here a hundred years ago."
He fluttered his eye lashes at the startling impossibility of
request.

"Mr. Gallo keeps a very tight schedule," he apologized.

So I followed a pace behind him, trying to gain my bearings
building I once knew well. Clearly a whole lot of crumpled
from the Sunday basket had been spent on the conversion.
hing was done on the cheap. The crown-molded hallways
ned just plastered and newly painted and smelled of fresh
oap and beeswax. The gold brocade carpet sunk underfoot.
eigh, who spoke not a word as we walked, stopped at a door
ked "Chancellor's Office" and indicated with a nod that I
uld step inside. Job done, he turned and disappeared down
hallway.

A stunning young woman sat just inside the door at a desk
a sign that read "Kelley Morrissey, Administrative Assis-

"I hear you have a three o'clock meeting with our friend Billy," he said without salutation.

"And just how did you come by that particular piece of information?"

"If you don't think I know everything that goes on around
here, you're not as smart as you think you are, Cosmo. You'll be
wise to remember that, my friend."

"What's he up to?"

"I can't tell you more than this. Early today, your old nemesis
Bishop McTighue stormed into Gallo's office with a face redder
than a cardinal's capello. He was in there all morning. Maybe you
can put your keen investigative skills to work and find out what
that was all about."

"What makes you think it had anything to do with what
happened to Waterman?"

Don ignored my question altogether.

"I'll give you a little additional friendly advice. Use a little
of your Italian charm on Gallo's secretary, one Kelley Morrissey.
She is a very capable young woman."

This apparently straightforward conversation was giving me
a whole lot to process. Don was coloring outside the lines a little,
but being very politic in not spelling things out too much. He
would not imply, but would tell me enough that I could infer.
Even if he was being subtle as a serpent, I was reading him like
my morning horoscope.

Bruster was letting me know first of all that he considered
Gallo, and probably McTighue, his rivals, simply by asking me
to help him find out what was going on between them. He was
also betraying that Gallo had not told him what McTighue was
roiled about, so Gallo probably considered Don a rival too. He
was certainly not in the chancellor's confidence. It was not too
far a leap from there to figure out that Billy Gallo would not
be inclined to share his schedule with Don, but Don made it

abundantly clear that he knew Gallo's schedule, so he must have a little bird in that office whispering in his ear. He allowed me to draw my own conclusion about who his little bird was, but Don could have called Morrissey "capable" in front of Cardinal Cody's ghost without any eyebrows lifting. So he was also putting me on notice that if I tried anything behind his back he would know about it, so I'd better not. Finally, by his very obliqueness, he was warning me to be discreet. He said none of this outright. But I had gotten it all. If we were face to face I would not have restrained a wink this time.

"One thing I have to tell you straight out, Cosmo, is to watch out for Tom's new partner. He's Gallo's son-in-law, and anything you say to him you might as well say to Gallo himself. Look, I've got to go. Don't call me. I'll be in touch if I find out anything else you might need to know. And when all the dust settles, if it works out, you are going to owe me more than egg rolls at Wing Ho. I want a trip with my wife to Hong Kong. You'll be able to afford it."

He hung up, leaving me to puzzle over that last comment. Don couldn't possibly know about my deal with Waterman, could he?

Peter from AAA Locksmiths set off the intercom buzzer a moment later. He had a no-show in the neighborhood and took a chance that I might be here so he could pick up my keys. I told him he could leave the new keys with Marge at St. Martin's Inn and headed out for the Pastoral Center, thinking about Don's call, more confused than ever. The sidewalks had gotten slippery. People had shoveled but my path was glazed with ice and slick and dangerous. The snow had stopped and it was starting to get cold, really cold. Chicago cold.

CHAPTER SEVEN

High among nature's most unpredictable ar
predators is the Chicago driver. In good
come up quickly from behind, trying to in
hoping to bully you aside. If that doesn't wor
past and swerve back into your lane with inches to
challenging you to rear-end them. In bad snow the
in the streets and weave to discourage any delusi
them. On my drive to the Pastoral Center I foun
rounded by ranging packs of them, acting as if w
to drive me from the road and out of their path.
stopped, but everyone seemed to be using it as an
work early. Midday the trip down Clark Street
dral should be a twenty minute drive. Today it t
as long. By the time I got a begrudging mutter of
the attendant at the archdiocesan lot opposite the
squeezed into a space, I was running so late I hal
slid down the snow-covered sidewalks. The Pastoi
a good four blocks from the lot, at the corner of R
son where the former Quigley Seminary, my hig
mater, rose in all its glory. The snow on the wind
tresses made the old gothic edifice look like it h
from medieval Europe and set down in the heart
most expensive neighborhoods in Chicago. Just
wondered, that the Bentley dealership moved in ac
from the faithful followers of the poor carpenter's

I entered what used to be the lobby of the Mon

tant." Her hair was jet black, her sloe eyes danced with intelligence, and her clear skin was the color of paperwhite narcissus petals. She wore a minimum of makeup, just a little eyeliner and a whisper of glaze on her full lips. She was dressed very modestly in an ivory high-collar blouse closed at the throat with a tiny bow. Not a woman who needed to flaunt her sexuality. Beyond surface beauty lay a deep air of apparent serenity, a woman at peace with herself and with the world.

On the corner of her desk was taped a small green flower fashioned from folded paper. For some strange reason I gathered the impression that she may have put it there just for me. Maybe I wished she had. She looked up as I entered. Her smile was genuine and warm.

"Mr. Grande, I cannot tell you how anxious I have been to see you. I was worried the snow might have kept you from getting here at all."

Her unabashed enthusiasm surprised and delighted me. Not the reception I had been expecting, nor the one offered by the frosty front-desk sentinel and my walking guard, Mike Raleigh. Morrissey seemed vaguely familiar, and I scanned my memory trying to think from where, but then dismissed the possibility. Despite the age difference—I put her in her mid-thirties—I would not have forgotten that face. I didn't realize that I hadn't responded to her greeting until my awkward silence evinced a blushed from her.

"Oh! I am so sorry," she stammered. "How presumptuous of me. I should have waited for you to introduce yourself. But even without the name tag I would have known it was you."

I instinctively reached out to shake her hand. It was cool and soft, and I resisted the temptation to bend and kiss it, surely expecting to find it redolent of bath talc and honeysuckle and girlish innocence.

"I'm the one who should apologize, Miss Morrissey. It's just

51

that I have taken the peculiar notion that that we've met some-where before."

"I'm certain we haven't," she said, "But please call me Kelley."

"Cosmo."

Her smile deepened and she seemed about to say something in response when voices from Gallo's office directly behind her made it clear that someone was about to exit. Kelley stepped quickly from behind her desk, spun me around, grabbed my shoulders with both hands, and pushed me through the door-way I had just walked through and into the bathroom across the hall.

"Stay here," she whispered. "Lock the door until I come for you."

She seemed not the least bit flustered. That made one of us. I acted as if I had no choice and did just as I was told. I might knock the mustache off the biggest blowhard in the bar, but I've never been anything but putty in the hands of a pretty girl.

Leaning an ear against the door I could hear muffled voices but couldn't make out the words. One was a male voice. Then Morrissey said, loud enough for me to hear, "Safe driving in the snow, Bishop McTighue."

It was another few minutes before Kelley tapped at the door. When I opened it she blocked my exit with a firm hand on my chest.

"I told Billy you were delayed by security. He's been in a mood all day. Don't mention knowing McTighue was here, no matter what he asks. And let him do the talking." I was surprised that she called him "Billy." I doubted she did so to his face. "And try not to disagree with anything he says. Our good chancellor enjoys drawing people into arguments."

Not the first time today I'd been given that particular warn-ing. Kelley led me out of the bathroom, back into the office, and went and tapped on Gallo's door. Before she opened it she said to me, "We'll debrief."

We walked into the room and Billy Gallo forced a smile as he stood up from his desk.

"Thank you, Kelley," he said dismissively.

The chancellor's office wasn't very big, though probably as close in size to the cardinal's office as any in the building. The exquisite mahogany and brass furnishings more than made up for its lack of spaciousness. It had that worn-leather, velvet-drapery feel of an exclusive men's club. Volumes of books more likely chosen by his decorator than his bibliographer. Paired lithographs of top-hatted English gentlemen and ladies ahorseback riding a star-crossed fox to ground. Gleaming brass sconces on the walls. The only things missing were a Waterford decanter half full of amontillado and a gentleman's gentleman patiently awaiting further instruction. The room was untainted by any likeness of our Lord and Savior—or even his designated vicar on earth.

Gallo came around his desk and extended a big, meaty ham of a hand at me.

"So good to see you again, Mr. Grande."

We'd never met, but I nodded and returned the handshake silently. He pointed to two burgundy leather love seats facing each other in the far corner of the office, lit by recessed lamps almost hidden in the ceiling. He waited until I sat down and then settled his ample frame directly across from me in the other. That's a dance he's done before, I thought to myself.

Gallo had the look of a former athlete gone to fat. No matter how many pounds they've put on, they never seem to lose their sportsman's bearing. He still had a thick coif of iron-gray, razor-trimmed hair, a pair of dark eyebrows almost joined in the middle, and light blue eyes I'm sure he thought of as penetrating. He was thirty pounds overweight, but the chalk-stripe charcoal suit fit him better than a banana peel, and the Balmoral Oxfords on his size-twelve feet were burnished to where they might offer a quick reflection up a Catholic girl's skirt. His white shirt was starched and looked uncomfortable and the striped tie would have probably told someone a lot smarter than me where he went to school.

The welcoming smile quickly faded. "I'm a busy man, Mr. Grande, so let's not dither about the weather. Tell me everything you know about the Waterman case."

"When did it become a case, Your Honor?"

"Cut the crap and tell me what you know."

"I don't think so, Billy," I said, as if disputing a point of fact, using his first name on purpose. "I would have to understand your interest in Mr. Waterman before sharing any...suspicions... I might have about his death."

The bell had rung. The fight had started. And we were both throwing exploratory jabs at each other. His ears started to turn red.

"I know all about you, Grande. I was hoping you still have enough love and respect for the church to want to avoid seeing her embarrassed in the newspapers once more."

"Once more?" I snorted. "Seems like every day there's another headline. Why should I care about exposing one more screwup?"

He shot his sleeves and adjusted the starched cuffs as if it were a job that suddenly needed to be done. He was a man unaccustomed to defiance. He seemed to be trying hard not to lose control.

"I have been hoping, frankly expecting, that you might feel a little pity for an ex-priest—and a former teacher of yours—who took his own life. A terrible thing. A mortal sin. Easing his family's pain might allow us to ease some of your burdens as well."

"What the heck does that mean?"

"I know that you are a person of interest in this case. You must know that I am not a man without influence. If you keep up with this baloney you're giving me I can make sure that the police maintain their interest in you and tell those newspapers you still read every day, and your licensing board, that you are a suspect in a criminal investigation. I can't imagine that would be very good for business."

Nothing about his words, or his tone, surprised or intimidated me. He sounded like all bullies sound. Here I was sitting on a $1,500 loveseat across from the chancellor of the Archdiocese of Chicago, the equivalent of the U.S. President's Chief of Staff, and hearing nothing but school-yard threats. The Italian in me started to rise.

They tell stressed-out public speakers to calm themselves by imagining that everyone they are addressing is naked. Me, I use my decades of Tae Kwon Do training in mental discipline. When stressed by someone, I find the deep pool of serenity at my spiritual center by imaging myself planting a sharp palm strike to the middle of the guy's fat face. Which I now took the opportunity to do.

"Do I amuse you, Mr. Grande?" he said with some exasperation. I realized then I must have been grinning. "Do you have nothing to say for yourself?"

"Sorry, Billy, I was somewhere else for a second there. I am back now. I do, in fact, have a couple things I'd like to say to you. First of all, why in the world would you think for a moment that I love a church that screwed me? Secondly, I haven't seen Ed Waterman since the day he kicked me out of Mundelein. Like I told the cops, including your son-in-law, by the way—oh, yeah, I know all about him. I haven't the faintest idea how Waterman got hold of my business card. I spread them around a lot." He tried to hide his reaction to my last comment with a soft cough into a closed fist. "Finally," I continued, "both of us know you won't go public, or even back to the cops, because you really don't know what I might have to say to them and it could, to use your words, cause one more embarrassment to the church."

The good chancellor folded his hands together over his crossed knees, as if composing himself or considering changing tacks. "Perhaps I came on too strong, Cosmo," he said, almost apologetically. "I'm sorry if I did. But you have to understand that we are under a lot of pressure here. You are insisting that you don't know anything about all this. All right. I choose to believe you. The archdiocese has lost a great champion of the faith in Ed Waterman, that's all, and we're sorry that no one here saw the obvious pain he was in and tried to help him. Enough then said about that."

Gallo stood up, walked across the room, and opened the symmetrical doors of a tall mahogany cabinet.

"What's your poison, Cosmo. I know you're a drinking man."

He pulled out Johnny for himself. Waterman would have been proud. I repressed the urge to ask for a snifter of amontillado.

"Any Jack Daniels?"

"Whiskey, yes. Sour mash, regrettably no."

"Anything brown."

He peeled the seal from a fresh bottle of Koval Four Grain and poured me a couple fat fingers in, yes, a tumbler of Waterford crystal. I lifted it in a toast and said, "Here's to the late Ed Waterman. May he rest in peace."

I was surprised by Gallo's loud "Amen."

What followed was small talk intended to lull me into thinking he was done with me. He wasn't really very good at it.

"You must find your work very gratifying," he said lamely. "Very interesting. Are you working on any interesting cases now?"

"It's kind of like hearing confession. I can't really talk about them. It's a different kind of priesthood than the one I hoped for."

"It is kind of a brotherhood, isn't it? Do you ever see any of your old classmates?"

Like I didn't know exactly where he was going, and why he was going there.

"I run into old classmates every now and then. Not usually on purpose."

"How about Mundelein faculty? I would think many of them must still be around."

"Not so much. You get thrown out on your ear, they don't usually look you up after."

With all the disinterest he could muster he asked, "Have you kept in touch with Bishop McTighue?"

"In Tulsa?" I said incredulously.

"He remains quite active in national church issues and often visits Chicago. He was just here. I'm surprised you didn't pass him in the hall."

"Can't say that I've had the particular pleasure of seeing him again."

My words seemed to signal the end of the interrogation. He had delivered the shot across my bow. Before I could finish what was in my glass, Gallo stood and put out his hand.

"Good seeing you, Cosmo. I appreciate your coming in on such short notice. Take care."

His long arm went around my shoulder and guided me firmly to the door. When it opened, Kelley was standing at her desk with her coat on.

"I hope you don't mind, Mr. Gallo. With all the snow I thought I'd get an early start home. The El is going to be jammed. I can walk Mr. Grande out."

"On your way, Kelley. If it snows anymore tonight, just stay home tomorrow."

Without another look at either one of us he turned and was gone.

Kelley looked at me as if in quiet assessment. "How about

a ride to Evanston?" she said cheerily. I took the notion that the idea had not just occurred to her. "I know it's a little out of your way, but I told you I'd like to hear what happened in there, and I know a few things that would be of interest to you. In fact, you should probably buy me dinner. We have a lot to talk about."

A lot to talk about? I thought. What the hell do we have to talk about? But a feeling long dormant inside of me, the notion that I have never had any hope against the will of a confident woman, told me we'd be dining out tonight.

"It'll be my pleasure." I said, wondering by what mocking twist of fortune that could possibly turn out to be true.

CHAPTER EIGHT

I offered to bring my car from the cathedral lot to the front steps of the Pastoral Center so she wouldn't have to walk through the slush, but Kelley demurred. So, heads down and walking into the weather, we made our way silently to the car. The wind howling around the buildings would have made any attempt at conversation difficult. When we reached the car she helped me brush away another inch of new-fallen snow with her gloved hands.

It wasn't until we got on Lake Shore Drive and the heater kicked in that either of us spoke. Traffic was moving slowly, but was at least moving. The plows had been working on the Drive without a break. I tried to hit the windshield with washer fluid, but the pump hummed in futility. Dead empty. The wipers themselves should have been replaced two winters ago. A hazy layer of salt was building up on my windshield, and it was like driving from the inside of a frosted light bulb. But with Kelley sitting next to me, I thought it better not to curse. So I just drove on. She was the one that broke the ice, so to speak.

"How can you even see where you are driving, Cosmo?" Her laugh made her sound more indifferent to the danger of riding with me than she probably was.

"Instinct, my dear, pure instinct." I regretted the "my dear" as soon as it was out of my mouth. "Pinball wizardry, Chicago-style," I went on, hoping she hadn't noticed, or would ignore it. "Haven't lost a passenger yet."

"There's a first time for everything," she said, wiping condensation from my side of the front windshield, and then from her own.

"You said dinner. Do you have a favorite place?"

"Not really. How about you?"

"After a half hour with Billy Gallo, any place with a full bar works for me."

"How about the Heartland Café on Morse? It's on the way."

I knew it well. An old hippie joint in Rogers Park that combined organic tofu, artisanal lettuce, fair-traded coffee, and all the left-wing politics you and your comrades could stomach. She noticed that her choice made me smile.

"What's so funny about that…my dear?"

Not a lady who missed much.

"I used to be a regular there a really long time ago, in a different life. My life changed and the place just sort of fell off my map."

"I had an idea you might know it. You do give off a kind of unreconstructed hippy air."

I winced. Traffic crawled. I had made a conscious decision not to ask her why she shoved me into the bathroom, and why she was in the car with me now, and why we were on our way to having dinner. She obviously had an agenda. I would let her unfold it in her own time. Keeping my mouth shut at the right time has sometimes been my finest investigative tool. People want to tell their stories, if only we will listen. I turned on the car radio.

"So, what kind of music does the administrative assistant of the chancellor of the Archdiocese of Chicago like to listen to?"

"Don't laugh, but I'm into the old stuff. Acoustic Dylan, Motown, Linda Ronstadt, the Eagles, Gram Parsons, Creedence. It's the stuff my mom played all the time when I was growing up."

"She's another unreconstructed hippy, I take it?"

"Was," she said.

Kelley got quiet after that. We were lucky enough to find a parking space right in front of the Heartland. We were a little early for the dinner scene and way late for the lunch crowd.

A dour young woman who looked like an unpublished poet moonlighting as a waitress seated us. The metal ring through her bottom lip made me wonder how she kissed anyone without drawing blood. Her hair was shaven on one side and teased on the other in a high blue rooster comb. I didn't get it. It's the kind of thing that grinds at me lately, these dots that I just can't connect. It made me feel that maybe I was too old to be sitting where I was sitting, across from a truly attractive woman, so much younger than me.

My instincts told me to just shut up and check out the menu. There wasn't a lot that looked good to an unapologetic carnivore like me. Our unpublished poet trudged back over to our table like she was walking through the snow outside. She looked first at Kelley, who ordered a grilled cheese sandwich and an iced tea. The waitress poised her pen over her pad and looked my way expectantly.

"How edible is the vegetable burrito? I asked.

She shrugged and looked at me like I asked her the cube root of 147.

"I didn't picture you for a vegan," Kelley said.

"I'm just trying to eat healthier these days. Let's do that," I said. "And a bottle of Frank's Hot Sauce if you got it."

"Would you like anything to drink?"

Oh, honey, if you only knew. Across the room the long rows of liquor bottles and the ranks of taps rising like crown jewels above the bar sang my name.

"Something that's good for you," I said.

"That would be the decaf herbal tea," she said, and padded away.

I was getting a little tired of Kelley's cat and mouse, so I finally broke down and asked, "So why'd you lock me in the men's room?"

"How about if I ask the questions, Cosmo," she said smiling, "Dinner was my idea, after all." Kelley's grin was accompanied by that blush of hers. "You really are still clueless about who I am."

"'Kelley Morrissey, administrative assistant,'" I said, wagging my finger as if at the name plate on her desk. "You see, I'm an experienced detective."

"Do you have no idea whose daughter I am?"

"How could I know that?"

"My maiden name is Sullivan. But I doubt that'll help you."

I returned her look with a blank stare. The only Sullivan who came to mind was a guy I had helped send to Statesville for robbing and killing an old lady on her way home from midnight Mass on the Southwest Side. Sullivan got shanked the first month he was locked up by another inmate who had just come to Jesus himself. No way could *that* Sullivan have been her dad. Kelley was enjoying her little game of I've Got a Secret too much to be tied to all that.

"Let's try this. I'm sure the name Margaret Hackett will ring a bell."

I could conceal neither my recognition of the name nor the confusion it caused me. I think my jaw dropped like a cartoon canine showing surprise. She clapped her hands together and laughed aloud at my obvious befuddlement. Kelley's mother was Peggy Hackett, the violet-eyed girl of my dreams who got her fill of me so many years ago, packed her bags, and left me and my broken heart in San Francisco.

"That's right," she laughed. "You're sitting across from Peggy Hackett's little girl."

The waitress brought our food as I sat in stunned silence. Absently unrolling my set up, I knocked a fork onto the floor but just let it lie. I couldn't stop staring at Kelley. I understood at last why she looked so familiar and why she felt comfortable copping an attitude with me.

No wonder she liked "the old stuff" as she had called her mother's favorite music. Before we skulked west, Peggy and I spent most free nights at the Earl of Old Town or Somebody Else's Troubles or the Green Mill or Ratso's or the Quiet Knight or Orphans, wherever there was live music—rock, blues, or folk. Bonnie Kolac, Mitch Aliotta, Haines and Jeremiah, the Rotary Connection, Steve Goodman, John Prine, Corky Siegel. They all made for a great time and a cheap date—usually with no cover. Those were unforgettable times, parked all night on a couple bottles of two-buck Pabst Blue Ribbon and listening to music that was just being born. My heart started to overflow with memories.

"You said 'was,' before," I said to Kelley.

"Huh?"

"When you mentioned her in the car, you said 'was.'"

Kelley's bright smile faded. She replied softly, looking down at her plate.

"Mom died two-and-a-half years ago. Just a month before my wedding. She had ovarian cancer. She fought it. Fought it hard, Cosmo. You knew her as well as anyone. Came to my fitting so she could see me in my gown and had a barf bag on her lap the whole time. When the pain got really bad I sat with her a lot. She enjoyed talking about her life, about what she did when she was young. Talking about the past seemed to carry her away from her pain somehow." She looked up at me with those dark eyes. "She talked about her time with you a lot." Kelley let out a deep sigh. "She made me make a promise before she died. And I am keeping it now."

I looked deeper into her eyes and then had to look away. I knew what I had to ask her even if I wasn't sure I wanted to hear the answer. I did the math in my head and calculated the possibility. I tried to look her in the eye but found my gaze flickering away from hers.

"Oh, sweet Jesus, Kelley!" I blurted out. "Are you telling me I'm your father?"

CHAPTER NINE

Kelley slammed her hands on the table so hard that the impact knocked my cup of herbal tea mercifully over my untouched burrito. She let out a burst of laughter that sounded like an ancient Celtic war whoop. I felt like a guy who just told the funniest joke in the world, except the joke was on him. Gasping for air she blurted out, "I think I'm going to wet my pants" so loud that every head in the restaurant turned and looked at us. Our waitress rushed over in alarm.

"You all right?" she asked, staring at Kelley, who appeared to be hyperventilating.

All Kelley could do was shake her head up and down and make mute gestures while producing a strange guttural sound. I was beginning to suspect I might not be her father after all.

"I think she got a bad bite of my burrito," I said to the waitress. "But she'll be fine. Just the check, please."

Kelley was trying hard to pull herself together. It took her a number of attempts before she could look at me without starting to laugh uncontrollably again. Finally, after taking a deep breath to compose herself she said, "You should have seen your face, Cosmo. I really thought you were going to faint."

"You never actually answered the question."

"Relax. I am definitely not the product of any wild oats that you may have sown in your drugged-out, hippie youth."

Sylvia Plath walked past our table and dropped our check atop the tea/burrito combo congealing on the plate in front of me. I decided I'd had enough for one day.

"Let's get out of here before I get us kicked out," Kelley said.

━━━

By the time we had cleaned the fresh snow off of my windshield and settled into the car I was able to smile about the entire scene myself, despite my embarrassment. I must have looked really foolish. Still, I found conflicting waves of emotions washing over me: initial terror, confusion, relief. But there was a hard dose of disappointment too. Finally, there was more than a little sorrow at the loss of Peggy. Old scars don't bleed, but they do remain forever.

I decided to drive up Clark into the south end of Evanston. The snow fell in a fine powdery mist creating soft cones of amber light at every street lamp, making the world look, for just this moment, magical and clean. We drove past the long rows of tombs at Calvary Cemetery. The gravestones and trees were iced with layers of soft snow that looked both pristine and surreal.

"You're not a Sullivan," I said. "You're married, then?"

"Used to be. He's a cop. Didn't work out. We were married less than a year. I started working for the archdiocese after I got the divorce. Mom had a friend, Don Bruster, who set me up in the job with Billy Gallo."

She did a little double take at my obvious reaction to the mention of Don's name, but before I could ask her about him she slipped off her seat belt at a light in front of Whole Foods.

"I need to get some food for me and my cat in case I get snowed in tomorrow. I'll jump here." She opened the door. "Don't worry. I can walk to my place from here. I really am so glad I finally met you, Mr. Cosmo Grande. We'll talk again tomorrow."

A quick pat on my shoulder and off she went. I didn't move at first, even when the light changed. Who buys cat food at Whole Foods when Jewel is just a block away? I figured she must be anxious to get away from me. Or from questions about her relationship with Don Bruster. The driver in the car behind me tapped his horn gently to get my attention. That's how they do it up here in Evanston. A mile south in Chicago there would have been a ten-second horn blast, flashing lights, a rolled-down window, a heavenward-pointing middle finger, a squeal of tires as the inconvenienced driver sped around me, and a heartfelt suggestion at full lung that I perform an unnatural act.

Kelley disappeared into the store. I drove around the block and headed back into the city. Clark Street would take me right home. Don's land line number was on my autodial. He had explicitly told me not to call, but I had questions, lots of them. I tripped into voice mail and decided not to leave a message.

I remembered that I had to pick up my new house keys from Marge at St. Martin's. I swung east on Devon to Broadway and allowed myself a smile. I had an excuse to have a short visit with Jack and clear the cobwebs in my head.

——

I gulped that first quick one—rules are rules—and cozied up real comfortably to a soothing second, but when it was dead I decided to call it a night. I settled with Marge, whose children are being educated on my dime, and left. I was driving just blocks from the bar when my cell phone rang. I figured at first it might be Don returning my call but it was a number I didn't recognize. It was Kelley. She wasn't laughing anymore. She didn't even say "Hello." She just started talking, struggling to stay calm and sound matter-of-fact. I wondered only later where she had gotten my cell number.

"Cosmo, I'm next door at a friend's condo. When I got home the doorman gave me a letter that someone had hand-delivered. So on the elevator I opened it and all it had printed on it in big black letters over and over again in all caps with no punctuation like a crazy person had written it, was DONT GO THERE DONT GO THERE DONT GO THERE, all over the page. When I got to my apartment I found the door closed but unlocked, and the lights were on all over the place. There was a plush stuffed kitten under water in my bathroom sink. And Mom's old bible was taken from next to my bed and left on an ottoman with a page torn out of it."

"Are you okay?" I whipped my car across oncoming traffic in a sweeping U-turn and got a warm Chicago welcome for it.

"Not hurt, if that's what you mean. Not sure about okay."

"The cat?"

"Purring on my lap."

"Did you call the police?"

"You are the first person I thought to call."

"Call them right now. I'll be right over."

"No. Don't. I'll be fine. They're having my locks changed in the morning and Sausalito and I are staying with my friends next door tonight. Nothing was taken."

"Sausalito?"

"Yah, I still have Mom's old cat. Listen, Cosmo, I'm fine. I just didn't want you to hear about it later and think I was holding out on you. Someone is just trying to scare us is all."

"Us?"

"Gotta go, Cosmo. I'll call you from work tomorrow if I go in."

She hung up before I could ask her anything else.

I debated going over anyway, but realized I didn't have her address. And after just two Jacks I was still sober enough to make a good decision and swung towards home.

Despite the relentless snow and all the snow-related parking restrictions, I pulled up to my building just as someone else was pulling out. Sometimes it's better to be lucky than to be good.

I was relieved to make it home. The new key slipped into the lock and slid the tumbler smoothly. When I opened the door two very hungry and very peeved cats yowled at me. I looked around. Nothing had been touched. No new voice mails. No new emails. Just as I went to sit down, I cursed and slapped myself a good dope slap for having forgotten the kitty litter and, more importantly, a replacement for the bottle of Jack poured down my sink. It was a toss-up between the cats and me as to who was most disappointed. Maybe staying clearheaded tonight was meant to be. I did have a lot of sorting out to do.

My cell phone rang. Caller ID told me it was Don.

"What's up, Cosmo? My call log says you were trying to reach me."

"Sorry, I know you told me to wait for your call, but—"

"Don't worry about it. What's going on?"

I started with the break-in at my place, which solicited no more than an "Oh my!" from him. Then I told him all about my meeting with Gallo. My description of it got a "Good, good" response from him. I told him about Kelley shoving me into the bathroom to avoid McTighue. He laughed at that. I decided to skip all the personal stuff from dinner and ended by describing Kelley's last call.

"I am completely confused, Don. Too many intersecting lines. I am lost here, and I know you know more than you're telling. You have to let me know how the dots connect, and soon, especially if you know what happened to Waterman or think that Kelley is in danger."

I shut up then and left the silence hanging. He seemed to be considering whether to be forthright. Or, more probably, just how forthright to be.

"All right, Cosmo. Tomorrow morning. Seven o'clock. Meet me in the basement book store of Old St. Peter's downtown. Come alone. The lights will be off. Just push the door open and head for the back. Be on time for a change. We won't have time to spare. Take the El, and if you have the slightest feeling that anyone has followed you, you must not come down the stairs. Just go into the church and make it look like you were going to morning Mass, that's all. I can't stress it enough. Don't come down the stairs if there is any chance you've been followed. Got it?"

"Yah, Don, I come down to the book store no matter who's following me."

That at last drew a little break in the tension in his voice. He said a little more warmly, "You really are a good friend, Cosmo. I know I can trust you. And know this. You *will* get some answers, I promise. And don't worry about Kelley. I've already got eyes on her."

"How'd you manage that?"

"Like I said, things will be a lot clearer after we talk in the morning. Meanwhile, get a good night's sleep. I need you at your sharpest. Maybe it's not so bad that your booze got poured down the drain." He laughed and hung up after a quick but sincere, "Sleep well, good friend."

I put down the phone, highly doubting I was going to get the kind of sleep Don wanted me to get. I had too many questions swirling in my head, and nary an answer. How could he already have someone watching Kelley? I was her first call, she had said, no more than twenty minutes ago. And I was absolutely sure I hadn't told anyone about the sad loss of my Tennessee sour mash. I fired up a half-burned blunt and took a couple of tokes, just to knock the ragged edge off a tough day, set my alarm for 5:30 a.m., and steeled myself for whatever lay ahead.

CHAPTER TEN

I tossed in and out of sleep all night, checking the clock every few hours, and finally woke to the sound of WBBM Newsradio telling me that yesterday's snows had passed and that nothing but clear skies lay ahead. The bad news was that I'd be walking to the Addison Street El with a wind chill hovering around five below. I set to my morning forms. Not that I was in any mood for it, but Tae Kwon Do is a kind of discipline, one that has kept me on the sunny side of a total ass-kicking more than once. Feeling petulant about how Don's mysterious request for an early meeting would be forcing me out into the pre-dawn cold put a little extra juice into my workout. The cats hid under the sofa while I lunged and yelled.

The sidewalks on the east side of Wrigley Field were deserted. Not even half were shoveled. The sudden icy snap on the heels of a warm, wet snow made for tough sledding, and I stumbled across the uneven ruts, all frozen rock hard. I passed not a soul walking down the dark street, but somehow, as if risen from the frozen ground, there were a hundred brave souls waiting with me on the El platform, all of us waddling in layers of apparel and pinching our faces in a pained expression, abiding, as we do here in Chicago, whatever next presents itself to be abided. When the train pulled in and the doors opened there still were a few seats available for the fleet of foot. I commandeered one in the corner of the last car. The heaters were working for a change, and no one seemed to be watching me with larcenous intent. It was a good start, maybe even a good omen, for the day ahead.

Past Fullerton the train slipped underground. By the time I got off at Monroe and walked up from the station, the sun was starting to shorten the dark shadows. It was officially morning. I was surprised by the number of people who were on the street as I headed west towards St. Peter's. When I got to the church I was even more startled to see so many people up and out of their warm beds early enough to catch Mass before going to work. I guess that worship, like my Tae Kwan Do, is a kind of spiritual discipline too.

I waited just inside the front doors until I was sure there was no one else around, followed the sign down the stairs and down the hall to the book store and gift shop. It did indeed look all locked up, just as Don said it would be, but I put my hand on the doorknob and pushed my way in. I found myself in a dark store. I looked back one more time to make sure no one had seen me sneak in. The staircase and hallway behind me were empty as bare ruined choirs where late the sweet birds sang.

I closed the door and locked it behind me, as instructed. As my eyes adjusted to the dark I took a moment to survey what I could see and noticed a band of light coming from under a doorway marked "Private" at the back of the store. I walked past mute statues of Francis of Assisi, Mother Theresa, and Padre Pio, framed pictures of popes, hundreds of crucifixes of all styles and sizes, decades of rosaries in glass, onyx, coral, and buffed olive wood. For a book store, it seemed to be painfully shy of books. I heard voices coming from the back room. They stopped when I tapped on the door. It was swung open by Don Bruster himself, proffering a cup of coffee.

"Cream, no sugar," he said. Just the way I take it.

"Hey, who's the detective here?" I said.

He leaned into the darkened store and looked in the direction from which I had come. "Alone, I trust."

"Me and all my friends."

I looked around the room behind him as he stepped back out of the doorway. Seated at a small conference table were six older men I had never seen before, looking very much like members of an exclusive club. It wasn't so much that they looked alike. Physically they were not at all similar. But there was something familiar about them that I couldn't at first put my finger on. With their smiles and nods, they gave out no vibes that threatened me in the least. Don pointed to an empty chair at the far end of the table. I sat down and shrugged my coat onto the back of the chair. Don stood at the other end of the table and began to speak.

"Cosmo, let me begin by saying that we are very sorry about all the cloak and dagger stuff, but experience has taught us that we have to be careful. You are the first outsider to ever be invited to an executive committee session."

He looked around the room and introduced everyone at the table by name, occupation, and diocese. I was trying to sniff out that common thing I sensed about them. Each was a Catholic permanent deacon. Two were the assistant chancellors of their diocese. Another was the head of the Marriage Tribunal of his diocese. Two others were the chief financial officers of their diocese. And the last one worked as the assistant to the president of the United States Conference of Catholic Bishops.

"And just what," I asked, "are you gentlemen the executive committee of?"

The deacon sitting to my right, who was from Atlanta, said, "I don't suppose the name 'The Knights of St. Thomas' means anything to you?"

Don smiled at the question. I took a sip of my coffee.

"Sorry. I haven't read a lot of Dan Brown novels."

"Better that you haven't heard of us," Don said. "We prefer to work outside the limelight."

He refilled his own coffee cup from the thermal pitcher in the center of the table. It finally hit me what it was that made these guys seem alike. It was power, not the kind you brag about, but the kind you wield. They all had an air of self-assurance about them that was as crisp as Billy Gallo's starched shirt collars. They were men not used to being told "no."

"The Knights of St. Thomas are a group of over one hundred permanent deacons from around the country," the Atlanta man explained. "We come from a variety of backgrounds and professional histories. To sit on this particular executive committee you have to be retired from your secular occupation and have agreed to dedicate yourself to working full time for the church. All our members are sworn to secrecy. We formed the Knights about ten years ago when we felt that we were being patronized and our considerable talents were being ignored by the new breed of bishops Rome was sending us. They all seem to be cut from the same cassock, unfortunately. Without a doubt the sex abuse scandal, the cover-ups, the growing number of not-very-pastoral priests being ordained, the curse of clericalism, were some of our initial concerns. But the looming scandal of financial irregularities, which we have found in more than one diocese, has become our paramount concern. It threatens to bring the Catholic Church in America to its knees."

"We love our church," an Hispanic deacon from Tucson, a slender, white-haired man who looked like someone's beloved *abuelito*, broke in. "At first we thought all we had to do was create the positive and professional environment so often lacking in the church. But now we find ourselves in way over our heads. We've uncovered some very disturbing financial arrangements. Criminal arrangements. This is why we have to keep our existence a secret. What has been unfolding in front of us these last few years has forced us to take mind-numbing precautions. Believe me, Mr. Grande, if we didn't have complete trust in Don you wouldn't be sitting here this morning."

Don tipped his coffee cup in salute to his compatriot and picked up where he had left off.

"We can't go into specifics with you just yet, Cosmo, but I will tell you, in a nutshell, that we have been scrutinizing church finances, and when we find 'irregularities'"—putting air quotes around the word—"we try to nudge the powers that be to take appropriate action. When they do, we count it among our successes. But more and more the powers that be have *become* the problem. Like it or not, we find ourselves trying to protect the church from some of the very people leading it."

Don paused and a deacon with one of those "pahk the cah in Hahvahd yahd" Boston accents spoke. "What we have uncovered so far makes my old nemesis Cardinal Law look like a saint. There is dark money, a lot of it, and keeping it secret has led to misfeasance, graft, lies, blackmail, threats, even violence, even bombings. You know who has a reputation for all of that."

"The RNC?"

"Come on," said the oldest of the group. "You're Italian, aren't you GRAHN-day? You're from Chicago. I'm talking about organized crime, the syndicate, the mob, the outfit. What else do you call it around here?"

It's not for nothing that it says "Private Investigator" on my business card. I thought I might have just detected a clue.

"Ed Waterman was up to his elbows in whatever you uncovered," I proffered.

"We have situations developing in Chicago and in another diocese that are rapidly coming unraveled," Don said. "We've kept them under wraps for close to a year, hoping to resolve them without a public scandal. Your investigation threatens to throw a spotlight on the whole mess. He told several of us that he was going to go to you before he ended his life."

"That's not something I can talk about."

"That's all right. We didn't bring you here to interrogate you."

"So why am I here?" I asked.

"We're old friends, Cosmo," Don said. "You and I trust each other. Everything the Knights do in our mission to protect the church depends on deep personal trust. Today we just need to know whether you are on board. That's all."

"You can trust me to do what's right," I said. "If that's what you're asking of me, fine, sure, I'm on board with that."

"Of course it's the same thing." He couldn't stop himself from looking around the room for some tell, some fidget, some sign of reluctance among his peers to do only what was right. I saw nary a flinch on any of the faces around the table.

"Trust us. Trust Tom Keystone. Trust Kelley Morrissey. They are working closely with us."

"So what do you expect from me?" I asked, looking around the table at each of them in turn.

"Sit quietly until you hear from one of our people," Don said. "It could be in a couple of hours or it could be in a couple of days, but we'll be in touch and you'll need to be able to move both quickly and cautiously. Stand and wait now, act quickly when action is required of you. We ask no more than that."

That seemed to be the signal for me to leave. I stood and slipped into my heavy coat. "I understand you guys have your secrets," I said. "But let me ask the one question that begs to be answered: What makes you so sure Ed Waterman's death was a suicide?"

None of them spoke for a minute. They looked around the table at one another like they were trying to decide who should answer. Finally the man from Atlanta looked me in the eye and said, "We believe it because the alternative is unthinkable."

CHAPTER ELEVEN

When I stepped into the street the morning light glaring off the snow momentarily blinded and disoriented me, forcing me to stop in my tracks. The phone in my pocket buzzed. Kelley.

"Yah," I said.

"Hello? Cosmo? Are you there?"

"Yah," I grunted again.

"Did I wake you?"

I laughed. "I had an early meeting. I've been up since five."

"The early bird catches the worm, I guess."

"All's I caught was a cold. What's up?"

"Listen. Gallo has cancelled all his appointments and taken a personal day. He told me not come to the office. It was like an order, not a suggestion. Weird. Anyway, I thought we could spend some time looking at all three bibles, maybe figure out what's going on with them. Something, that's for sure."

"Wait a minute, Kelley. Just what do you know about the other bibles?"

"You really do crack me up. It's elementary, my dear Watson. Stop playing so dumb."

"What makes you so sure I'm playing?"

I turned and tottered gingerly on the ice towards the subway as she shifted gears.

"So, Cosmo, I'm thinking you could use some breakfast after your early morning meeting. I'll take care of everything. And I promise no vegetable burritos or herbal tea. I'll be at your place at ten sharp."

She hung up without bothering to hear if I concurred.

Gallo's behavior was curious. I pondered that one for a moment, but decided I was already drilling enough dry holes for six investigations. I wondered again how Kelley knew about the other bibles. Don had probably filled her in on our conversations. But he only knew about *my* bible. Maybe Kelley's. But how the hell did either one of them know about Waterman's? From Tom? He was the only other person who knew about it. That must be it. I dialed Tom.

He was all business when he answered.

"What's going on?" he snapped.

"I just came out of a meeting with Deacon Don Bruster and a few of his oldest friends."

I let it hang, waiting to hear what his response to that was going to be.

"I have no doubt it was a most interesting meeting," he said. "But you never called anyone to *give* information. What do you want?"

"I need to take a closer look at that fancy bible you found on the chair next to Waterman's bed."

"Fine private investigator you are. It wasn't left on his chair. It was on the footstool, the footstool, Cosmo. I'll get a radio car to drop it off. Let's say in an hour."

"The condo," I said. "Not the office."

He broke the connection.

The Chicago El is not the worst place to ponder the inscrutable. When you are running underground, there's nothing at all to look at out the windows. The rhythmic murmur of the wheels on the rails and the gentle rocking of the car can prove hypnotic. A lot of snoozing people lose purses, watches, or iPods because of it. But a whole world opens up when the train rises out of the tunnels and morphs from subway to elevated, lifting you from darkness into light.

When we emerged into the bright morning I saw below the tracks a few hardy souls shoveling their cars out of the drifts, and dirty snow piled by the plows against parked cars down the long streets. A uniquely Chicago winter tradition was starting to unfold, one that goes back so far that pundits argue when it began. Folks put out old kitchen or lawn chairs, empty garbage cans, disconnected toilets, whatever they find, to defend the spot they dug out of the snow in front of their homes. The Chicago parking chair represents an unspoken pact more faithfully honored than most international trade agreements, and failures in compliance are more strictly enforced.

I made it back home with half an hour to spare, even with a little detour to the package store for an essential resupply. When I walked in the cats stirred and looked confused. They probably thought I would be out for the day and had settled in a sunny corner.

I looked around my place and felt a sudden thrill of panic when I realized I had nowhere near enough time to sanitize the place before Kelley arrived. I started in the bathroom, by far the worst offender. I wiped the sink and toilet with dirty towels and threw them into the closet with the unwashed underwear that was lying on the floor. I had no time to scrub the layers of grime off the tub so I closed the shower curtain and splashed some Lectric Shave around the sink to mask the musty smell. I looked around. It looked minimally passable, grading on the curve.

I stopped in the kitchen and just scratched my head. I needed a plan, fast. Five minutes later a fifty-gallon heavy-duty garbage bag was filled with dirty litter from the cats' box, three weeks of old *Sun-Times*, the empty Jack Daniels and beer bottles my burglar had left in the sink, an assortment of Leona's pizza boxes, waxed Chinese take-out cartons, and Hormel Chili cans. I opened the refrigerator and threw out everything that failed a quick sniff test or bristled with mold. Then I left the bag, bulging, on my back porch. I used half a roll of paper towels to clean the stove, counter tops, and sink and then swept the floor. I hid the tilting piles of dirty dishes in the dishwasher that has been stone cold dead since the last time the Bears won the Superbowl.

In the living room I knew my desk was hopeless, so I just straightened the furniture, raising motes of dust and drifting clumps of cat hair. I decided just to close the door to my bedroom, another hopeless case. I gave it all a quick once over, thinking it looked pretty good for a bachelor pad. The doorbell rang. I looked at my watch. It was three minutes after ten. I ran my fingers through my hair and opened the door with a big welcoming smile on my face. Unfortunately, it wasn't Kelley. I had forgotten about the delivery of Waterman's bible. And it wasn't a uniformed cop either. There I was with a goofy grin on my face, staring at the kid, Tom's partner Andy, holding what looked like a small loaf of bread wrapped in a brown paper.

"This is from Tom."

He stood in the hallway looking contrite. I decided not to let him in.

"Thanks, Andy. It is Andy, isn't it?" The package in his hands had clearly been opened, inspected, and rewrapped rather sloppily. So the kid knew he was handing me Waterman's bible but probably had no idea why. Hell, I was pretty clueless myself.

"Thanks much, kid, and thank Tom for me."

Andy bristled at being called "kid" and turned on his heel. I took the package, turned around, and gently closed the door. I stood just inside listening. I expected he might be ticked off because I didn't give him a chance to scope my place out, and I didn't hear him move away on the other side. So I let out a loud "Aha! I knew it," just to throw him a curve ball. I walked to the living room window and waited. He came into view in a moment walking with determined steps to his unmarked squad car double-parked, police lights flashing on the dash, with four cars stuck on the street behind him. Just as he pulled away my land line rang. It was Kelley.

"Where are you?" I asked.

She had struck me as someone who, like her mother, was never late.

"I was just getting out of my car when I saw *Andy* walking up your steps. What does he want?"

"He's Tom Keystone's partner. He delivered Ed Waterman's bible like you wanted. Do you know him?"

"In the biblical sense," she said, much to my surprise. "He's my ex-husband, Andy Morrissey. We still have the same last name. Some private eye you are."

"Come on up. He's gone."

A minute later, I opened the door before she could ring the bell, grabbed one of the bags she was carrying and led her into the kitchen. We dropped the bags on the counter, and she took off her coat and folded it neatly across a chair. I was relieved that she hadn't tried to hang it in my closet.

"Sweet mother of all that is holy, this apartment is a disaster, Cosmo. Couldn't you have taken ten minutes and cleaned the pigsty up?" She may not have been my daughter, but she was most definitely Peggy's. "Leave me alone in here, will you? I'll find what I need or I'll just make do. While I fix breakfast why don't you try to figure out why Tom chose Andy as his delivery boy."

I went to the living room and paged through Waterman's bible. Soon aromas that I knew well but hadn't smelled for years were wafting from the kitchen. Peggy's insuperable onion, fennel, capers, and Fontina cheese omelet, my all-time favorite breakfast. Pretty soon I noticed the fragrance of cinnamon rolls baking in the oven. Kelley used her mother's old trick of putting a few drops of almond oil in the grounds when she brewed coffee, and in short order my musty bachelor pad was redolent of cinnamon and licorice and marzipan, and the long decades since I had Peggy in my life seemed to drift away. Both cats slipped out of hiding with their noses in the air, taking in all the unfamiliar scents.

Kelley sounded so much like her mother when she shouted "Come and get it, Cosmo," that I almost expected to find Peggy standing at the stove. The cats arched their backs against her calves and mewed and purred at her ankles while she loaded steaming plates of food. I looked at Kelley and my heart ached. If only I hadn't been such a *ciuccio* back in the day, I might have had a daughter like her.

"This brings back some happy memories," I said. "You have no idea."

"Mom made this breakfast every Christmas morning. She once told me it was your favorite."

We sat at opposite sides of my small kitchen table and I had a hot cinnamon roll in one hand and a forkful of omelet in the other when she made a quiet sign of the cross. I put my food back on the plate while she prayed.

"Lord, we thank you for the nourishment you have provided for our bodies this morning, for the memory of a woman who nourishes our hearts, and for the circumstances that have finally brought us together, and for cats," she said, "and for conundrums, and for all your blessings. Amen."

I muttered my own "Amen" and found myself stuck for a moment on the thought of blessings, those that I had let slip away and those that might yet lie ahead. We sat down quietly sharing the food Kelley had so carefully prepared in the manner of her mother and, I guess, some of the same sadness, and maybe some of the same hope, each in our own way.

CHAPTER TWELVE

When we had eaten until we could bear no more, Kelley stood and began to clear the table. "I'll clean up in here a bit and make fresh coffee. Leave me with these dishes and take a look at those bibles. See if you can figure out why they were damaged the way they were. It must be some kind of clue."

She seemed a little wistful, as if she might like a few minutes to herself. I was okay with that. I was feeling the same way.

I realized as I settled myself on the couch how easily an old tomcat like me could become domesticated. I unwrapped Waterman's bible. As I leafed through it I saw the fine residue from the fingerprinting still on it. The dark cover, the only likely place for the perp to have left prints, which had clearly been wiped clean, still had faint traces of fine white powder on it, probably a cocktail of kaolin and titanium dioxide. The inside pages were dusted with a micro-milled black powder. I blew it off as I paged through the book so that the delicate pages wouldn't get smudged. This book was more than a bible. It was a work of art, hand bound in a soft brown leather that was dark and supple. The pages were gilt-edged, and the many full-page illustrations inside appeared to have been hand colored. Waterman's name was neatly written in the upper right hand corner of the inside cover in black ink. It had been carefully handled but was clearly well read. It hadn't been sitting on a bookshelf or forgotten in a drawer, as most bibles are. That's why it was jarring that a page in Genesis had been roughly torn out and taken.

Peggy's bible was similarly desecrated. It was a soft-cover book, a translation that I had never seen before, published by a group called "Priests for Equality" and entitled *The Inclusive Bible*. Peggy's name was penciled on the bottom of the title page in her careless hand. The creased and dog-eared pages throughout proved that someone had read from it often. There were a number of memorial cards in it, the ones they pass out at funeral homes. Some Hacketts. Some Sullivans. I didn't recognize any of the individual names. I couldn't quell a secret hope to slip a card with Peggy's name on it into my pocket, but had no luck in finding one. A dried rose was pressed between two pages, and prayer cards and old photos were scattered throughout the book. Some pages had passages underlined or highlighted or notes written in the margins. I started to feel uncomfortable, like I was reading someone's secret diary. Fanning through the pages I noticed one torn page, ragged at the spine where it had been ripped, just like the missing page in Waterman's bible. I quickly checked. Hebrews 7.

I reached over to my desk for the chunky Jerusalem Bible that I had read since my student days in the seminary. J.R.R. Tolkien had been among its translators. Its distinctly literary voice far outshines every other contemporary translation, in my piety-impaired opinion. Paging through it now I had a pretty good idea what I was going to find. Sure enough, a page had been torn from two thirds of the way through the book of Psalms.

"Damn! This is starting to get personal."

"Who are you swearing at now?" Kelley walked into the living room carrying two steaming coffees and placed them on the table. She sat on the old recliner across from the couch, with one leg curled under her, just as her mother used to. She reached over and picked up her mug, cupping it in the palms of both hands, once again mirroring Peggy without being aware of it. She caught me staring at her.

"What?"

"Sorry. I just keep seeing a lot of your mother in you. It brings back a whole lot of memories that I thought were long gone."

"Good ones, I hope."

Before I could answer, my cell phone rang. I wanted to answer Kelley's question, and thought to ignore the phone until I saw that it was Don. I hadn't been expecting to hear from him so soon.

"Hey, Don. What's up? Kelley and I are just—"

"Listen to me, Cosmo. Something is breaking hard down here at the Pastoral Center. Nobody showed up for my nine-thirty meeting."

"I already heard Gallo was blowing the day off."

"The cardinal has cancelled all his appointments for the day. Says he's staying at the mansion shaking a flu bug. He was the picture of health at the Mercy Hospital Ball last night. What did Kelley say about Gallo?"

"Just that he cancelled everything and told her not to come in. She's right here. Do you want to talk to her?"

"She knows how to reach me if she needs to." Don lowered his voice. "McTighue is back, running around this place like a crazed primate looking for Gallo and the cardinal."

"Like an ooh, ooh, eee, eee, aw, aw primate or like a mitred primate?"

"A little of both," Don laughed. "He was screaming at every secretary and canon lawyer he could find. Even tried to button-hole me. He finally stormed out. Clearly he is not very happy. Maybe Kelley has some idea what got his boxers twisted."

"I'll ask her."

"Don't tell her this, Cosmo," he said, lowering his voice even further. "Her ex, Gallo's son-in-law, just came by here too. I think McTighue was already gone. Anyway, he started bugging people about McTighue, asking what the bishop was doing here.

Seemed like he had a suspicion, and was trying to confirm it. I ran him down and asked him where Tom Keystone was. That seemed to fluster him. I called Tom. He had no idea what the hell Morrissey was up to. Said if the kid was down here asking questions he'd gone rogue. Told me Morrissey told him he needed time off to take care of some personal business."

"There's a lot of that going around."

"What the hell is happening here, Cosmo?"

I took his question to be rhetorical. No one seemed to understand less about this case than me.

"Give me a chance to talk to Kelley," I said. "I'll get back to you. Let's stay in close touch. Don't go taking the day off."

Kelley had listened with intense interest to my end of the conversation.

"Someone gave an order to abandon ship," I said. "Don's staff is out and the cardinal has the flu."

"Gallo occasionally takes unscheduled days off, usually without much warning. I have to scurry to cover for him. But he's never ordered me to stay away before."

I decided to ignore Don's instruction to keep her in the dark about her former husband. We were opening up too many dark closets as it was, and I needed to shine light on something.

"Your ex made a beeline from here to the Pastoral Center. Didn't tell Keystone a thing about it. He was asking about McTighue."

"What has Bishop McTighue got to do with Ed Waterman?"

"And why is Andy Morrissey running him to ground? And trying to hide from his partner the fact that he is doing it?"

A thought seemed to cross her mind, but she apparently thought better of sharing it.

"So, what's his story?" I asked. "In fact, what's your story with him?"

Kelley hesitated, as if she wasn't sure she wanted to share, and then I caught a glimpse of that look of resolve her mother showed when the going got tough.

"You know talking about him will only tick me off."

"I don't mean to pry, Kelley. I'm just confused. It hasn't been five hours since I find out that you and Tom Keystone are hip deep in God knows what with a bunch of renegade deacons who fancy themselves knights. Then I learn that Tom's partner, married to the daughter of the chancellor of the archdiocese who you just happen to work for, is your ex-husband. I can't tell the good guys from the bad guys. I don't know who's telling me the truth and who's blowing smoke. I'm waiting for a message from a dead man, I might be on the trail of a murderer, and I could find myself facing down the Chicago mob, the Knights of St. Thomas, a rogue cop, a bishop or two, and Holy Mother Church herself. I need to get some clarity about *something*, Kelley, and you might be my only chance of getting it."

The expression of resolve I had caught in her eyes finally seemed to morph into composure, even confidence. She settled back, like someone getting ready to tell a long story.

"Andy changed," she began. "Things were great between us when he was at the academy, but after he got out on the street things just seemed to turn dark for him. He started taking a lot of wrong turns. The divorce was his idea, not mine, even though the relationship had soured long before. As soon as the papers were official, he started the annulment process. It came through from Rome surprisingly fast, I guess because the chancellor's daughter was waiting in the wings. Billy didn't seem too keen about the marriage from what little I heard, but he loved his daughter and beyond all the bluster he's not a bad guy. I was already working for him when my marriage to Andy went bust. In fact, as the divorce was unfolding, he took me aside and promised the job was mine as long as I wanted it. I'm not sure when he found out my ex and his daughter were getting serious, but he never brought it up and neither did I. It's a little awkward even now, but I suspect someone in the legal department told him the whole mess put me in a kind of protected class. Like it would look bad for him if I ever got fired. I'm pretty sure he never had even the slightest suspicion that Don pushed buttons to get me the job interview in the first place. Billy did the hiring, but I think Don made sure I was the only presentable candidate he talked to."

"I wondered about that. How did you and the Knights happen to connect?"

"As Mom's illness progressed, she found herself surrounded by lots of good priests and wonderful parishioners who really loved her and were concerned about her and helped her—helped both of us, really. They brought Mom, that old radical feminist from the 60s, back to the church. She found a real community for herself at St. Nick's. That's how we ended up in Evanston. The parishioners there affirmed her personally, all women in the church, really, in ways that most places never tried to.

"So I came to love the church and the parish for what it did for her, especially those last awful months. Now, if I can do something to keep the Catholic Church from self-destructing, I feel like I owe it to them, and to Mom, and maybe to myself to do it."

"You haven't answered my question about the Knights."

"I met Don when I helped organize a Catholic Charities golf outing. He and his wife quickly became my good friends. After Mom died, he suggested I apply to be Gallo's assistant and let me know it was a pretty sure thing. I came to understand very quickly that he had his own agenda in helping me. And frankly, the Mata Hari role has been fun, at least until all this craziness started." Her face clouded over just for a moment. Then she caught herself and smiled. "Look at it this way, Cosmo. How else was destiny going to bring Mom's great lost love into my life? You know the old saying, 'Through the eyes of faith, nothing is a coincidence.'"

I almost blushed at her words, and could not repress an impulse to redirect the conversation from my blemished past.

"You seemed distressed about almost running into Andy this morning. What's up with that? Still carrying a torch?"

She scoffed. "And you a private investigator? You couldn't be more wrong."

"You told me the divorce was his idea. It's not an unreasonable inference."

"I have never felt comfortable telling anyone this. But here it goes. Andy is dirty. His father was connected with people you just knew weren't square. Andy always bet on the Bears when we were dating, and never had trouble finding someone to take his bets—even the big ones. He got in way over his head and lost everything he had, then everything I had. That's why there was no mention of money in the divorce settlement. There wasn't any. When I was putting all that stuff down in the questionnaire, I knew the annulment was going to be a slam dunk. I don't know how much Gallo or his daughter knew. Gallo, probably everything. He can use it to hold over Andy. I'm sure he's still gambling. And whatever Andy still owes the mob, you can bet they're taking it in trade. Andy Morrissey is the private property of the Chicago syndicate."

CHAPTER THIRTEEN

Kelley and I turned our attention then to the mystery of the three bibles, Kelley on the easy chair with one leg crossed under her and me on the couch where I often spend the night.

"I know for sure," she said, "that there wasn't a ripped out page in my bible before the break-in. I'm going to venture a guess that you're going to say the same about yours. And I can't believe Waterman's was ever damaged before. So, we need to take a closer look at what we have here in front of us and what it is trying to tell us."

She was all business, focused with that intensity both she and her mother had on doing whatever needed to be done next. I confess that I wasn't as tuned in to the task at hand as she was. I was a little dismissive of the bibles, weighing larger issues. I noticed that Kelley had carefully removed the pressed rose from her bible and set it gingerly on the coffee table. That rose was special. Maybe it was a memento from Peggy's funeral. I tried to get myself to stop drifting into the past and focus on the three books in front of us.

"My first thought was that it was just a random act of desecration."

Without looking up at me she said, "I don't know, there's got to be something else here, some connection, some message. Back when you were in the seminary and weren't smoking up, they must have managed to teach you something about scripture. Figure it out."

Her cell phone chimed and she stroked open a text message.

"It's from Tom. The Knights are gathering the troops right away. I'm afraid I have to leave you to wash out your Mr. Coffee all alone. Think you can get it done before next Groundhog Day?"

I checked my cell phone. No messages.

"Why didn't I get a call?"

"You're not officially on board."

"Where's the meeting?"

She shook her head. "Telling you that would be so against the rules. Sorry. And without the password you would never be let into the space in the basement under the main chapel at St. Rita High School at 79th and Western anyway."

"Call me if you need me for anything, anything at all. I'll be nearby. And I never close."

She stood up wordlessly, leaned over, and gave me a big hug. She grabbed her coat from the chair and left, slamming the door behind her. I went to the window to watch her walk to her car. Kelley turned once and waved up at the window as if knowing that I would be watching her. She drove off, tires spinning to gain a little traction against the slippery surface of the street.

I fed the cats, bundled up, and skidded down the sidewalk to my car. The last night's snow had hardened into a shell of ice. It took me ten minutes scraping with an expired BP credit card to open port holes sufficient for the drive to St. Rita's.

When I finally sat in the car and turned the key to start it, I got not as much as a solenoid click. The battery was deader than Al Capone. I tried the lights and the radio and tapped the horn. Nothing.

I pulled out my cell phone and called Joey Greco's garage on Halsted, just a couple blocks away, to come and give me a jump. I fired a quick text to Kelley. "Car won't start. Stay in touch."

Joey pulled up in fifteen minutes with a big red plow attached to his new tow truck. I cracked the door open so we could talk.

"Hey, Cosmo. When are you going to replace this heap? One of the guys at the shop says its resale value doubles every time you fill the tank."

"Someone's got to put your kids through college."

"Pop it, eh?"

He took a quick glance at the engine compartment, slammed the hood closed, and then shook his head at me through the gap I had just scraped in the ice. He walked over to the driver's side and opened the door wider.

"You ain't going nowhere, buddy. You don't have a dead battery. You got no battery at all. It's been lifted. By somebody who knew what he was doing."

"Yeah, if he's so smart, why'd he steal a battery that was older than Larry King?"

"They didn't want the old one. It's prob'ly sittin' in a dumpster within three blocks of here. You park here all the time, right?"

"I live right there," I said, pointing to my building.

"They'll be back tonight to steal the brand new one I put in this afternoon. I see it all the time."

"What a world."

"Funny thing, though. They took the alternator too. I can't say I've seen that before. A kid on crack can pop a battery blindfolded in ten seconds flat, but an alternator takes time, and good light. A lot of exposure."

"What the hell?" were the only words I could muster.

"You know either of these guys?" Joey said, waving a finger at the two cars that had me hemmed in. Both were shuttered with snow.

I shook my head.

"I'll never get it out of here. Leave notes on their windshields and call me when I can get at it. I ain't fixing it in the cold."

I went back to the house for a pad and pen and a kitchen

chair. I cleared the windshields of the cars on either side of mine and left a note on each asking the owners to call me and to put my Chicago parking chair in the open spot when they left.

I was pretty well stuck at home until one of those cars moved, and wanted to be around when a space opened up. I turned my attention back to the bibles. Waterman's had a page torn from Genesis, mine from Psalms, Kelley's from Hebrews. Apart from the suggestion of randomness, which still got me nowhere, location of the missing pages told me nothing. It might be a red herring, a simple effort to misdirect my investigation. Like everything else about this case, I not only had trouble connecting the dots, I wasn't even sure where the dots were. What was going on at the Pastoral Center with Gallo, McTighue, the kid, and the cardinal? Who was trying to keep me from moving? And why had the Knights called an emergency meeting that I wasn't invited to? I was dead tired from a restless night and starting to get a monster headache. I decided a buzz might take the edge away and help me think more clearly. Yah, that's going to really happen. Who was I fooling? I just needed to mellow out for a while in a place where there were no questions without answers.

I rolled and fired a fresh joint, put on my earphones, started grooving to the Best of Creedence, and to tell you the God's truth, I never lost one minute of sleepin' worryin' 'bout the way things might have been.

———

I woke up with the Bose earphones pressing hard against my cheek and the CD stopped. I sat up, disoriented. As I pulled the earphones off, the message alert from my phone drew me fully awake. With the noise-blocking ear phones on I had apparently slept through a lot of calls, and the voice mail icon blinked with the numeral 6. I looked at my watch. It was a quarter to eleven.

I had to parse a minute to discern that that must be night, not morning.

The first message was a neighbor whose name I did not recognize telling me he got my note, had pulled his car out of the space behind my car and left my chair in it. The second was Joey asking if he could come and get my car yet. The next message was from Don, who said simply, "Call me the minute you get this."

Then there was a surprise message from Gallo, who wasted no time getting to the point. "Grande, if I find out that you have anything to do with what's happening, whatever the hell is happening, I'll feed your balls to the fishes. Got it? Call me. I need to know everything you know and I need to know it now."

It was actually kind of refreshing to hear from someone who was as confused as I was.

A fifth call was from Kelley.

"Thanks for the text, Cosmo. It's been a tough day but I made it home safe. I'm beat, and turning in now, so I'll call you in the morning." Almost as an afterthought, she added, like she was reminding me to pick up cat food the next time I went out, "I guess you heard about the bomb. Bye."

I didn't recognize the inbound number on the last message. Not a Chicago exchange. I didn't recognize the voice. The message was short and not so sweet. All that the guy on the other end said was, "We could have just as easily put a bomb under the hood of your car, big shot. Maybe there's one there right now. Back off or things start going boom."

When they threaten to kill you, now that's a good time to call the cops. I saw that Tom Keystone had called several times without leaving a message. I hit the last time his number registered and pressed "Call."

"About freaking time," he answered. "I'm headed for your place. I'm like three blocks away."

"What do you know about a bomb?"

"Threat. No bomb. St. Rita's School. What's that got to do with the price of potatoes?"

"I just received a bomb threat of my own. Some guy called and said my car might be wired."

"Where is it?"

"Right out front."

"Stay put. Don't even think about going near the car, or even coming outside. I'll have people there in five minutes."

I stepped to the window and looked out across the dark street to where my car sat with the hood still unlatched. Tom pulled alongside my car in a minute, then backed up about fifty feet and angled his car, flashers going, so it blocked the street. He got out and walked back past my car and stood blocking the other end of the street with a four-cell flashlight in one hand and his badge in the other. He shooed a few curiosity seekers, and in a few minutes a patrol car arrived and cordoned off a sixty-foot radius around my car with yellow tape. A Humvee rumbled down the street and a man with a dog got out and led the dog in an ever-tightening circle around the car. He let the dog sniff the tires and under the car and finally, shaking his head, led the dog away. While he was doing this another guy got out of the Humvee and suited up like the Pillsbury Doughboy. He walked all around the car shining a bright light on the ground, walking stiffly in his thick blast suit, paying particular attention to foot-prints in the snow. He circled the exterior of the car and inspected the undercarriage with a mirror on a stick, then shined his penlight into the interior for a long time. He finally popped both back doors with a stainless steel lever, just the way the neighbor-hood kids do, and spent another five minutes shining his light around inside. There was a knock at my door and a patrolman asked me to identify myself, and to give him the keys to the car, which I did. The guy in the street popped the trunk, inspected it, then opened the front doors, cracking them first and inspecting the hinge area. He last opened the hood, just an inch at first, and then all the way. He spent a long time looking and then walked towards the building out of my line of sight and then back. He leaned into the front driver side of the car a minute then backed away and closed the door. He finally lifted the big domed helmet from his head and shook it at Tom. Tom walked over and spoke to him for a moment then headed towards my building.

"It's clean," he said when I met him at the door. "Started right up."

"That's not possible," I said. "Someone stole the battery and alternator last night."

"And then brought it back tonight? What you been smokin'?"

"No really, wait."

I pulled out my phone and dialed Joey Greco's cell. "I have a witness," I said to Tom. "The son of an old friend who owns a garage. He saw it." Joey picked up after a couple rings. "Sorry if I woke you, Joey, but I got kind of an emergency. I've got a cop here who thinks I've lost my marbles, and I just need you to tell him exactly what you saw when you opened the hood of my car this morning."

I handed my phone to Tom, who listened a moment and simply ended the conversation with, "Thanks a lot, sir. Sorry to bother you in the middle of the night." Tom gave me a dark look without saying a word.

"So, do you believe me now?" I said, gloating a little at the restoration of my credibility.

"Your friend Joey says that he hasn't seen you or talked to you since you stiffed him on a set of four Michelin tires six months ago. He has no idea what you are talking about."

CHAPTER FOURTEEN

I'll confess that the fact that Tom didn't believe me hurt. He and I go back a lot of years. He took up a major chunk of space on my short list of friends and shouldn't have doubted I was being set up. He settled himself on the chair Kelley had perched on yesterday with a frown creasing his face.

"What am I supposed to think here, Cosmo?"

"This is crazy, Tom. I've known Joey since he was a kid. He wouldn't lie to hurt me."

Out in the kitchen I heard my brand new 1.75-liter bottle of Jack Daniels call my name, but I was still feeling a little fuzzy from the grass I smoked and kicking back a couple inches of whiskey was probably not going to help my current credibility problem. Tom just stared at me without as much as a glance down at the three bibles on the coffee table. Without thinking much about it I closed them and stacked them neatly together, still withering a little from Tom's apparent lack of faith in me.

It was noticing the pressed rose from Kelley's bible that somehow helped me flash on how I could assuage Tom's doubt. Maybe it was a gift from Peggy, who knows? What I did know was that I could prove my version of the story. Joey had phoned my cell, not the land line, and left a message I had not yet erased. I flipped to my archive of voice mails, tapped the speaker on and said, "Listen and learn, Detective." I tapped the play button on Joey's voice mail. Joey's voice came on, with his rig rumbling in the background.

"Yo, Cosmo. Your alternator's here. You get either of those

cars moved yet? I ain't changing it in the street in this friggin weather. Call me 'til seven. Otherwise it'll have to wait 'til tomorrow."

I held the phone up so he could see the date and time stamp. He frowned in puzzlement.

"Somebody got to him," he said, almost in relief.

Then I played the threat. His eyes widened a little at "things start going boom."

"You can't have known any of this," I said. "What brought you over here in the middle of the night?"

"It had to do with Andy. I got it from a friend in Internal Affairs that he's been seen with some mob soldiers. And there's a not unreasonable suspicion that the mob is involved with the Waterman case. The Knights figure that you are the guy who can find out about it, and they wanted me to say it to you in person so I could gauge your reaction. I figured you'd still be up nursing a bottle."

"I heard Andy was dirty."

"He wouldn't be the first cop in this city to go sour."

"So why did you send him here with Waterman's bible?"

"Give me some credit. I didn't send him. He told the cop I gave the bible to that he was heading up this way. I see he got it here."

"After taking a peek. He tried to rewrap it, but it was clear that he checked it out."

He nodded. "Do you think he had any idea pages were missing from all three bibles?"

"How did you know about that?"

"It came out in Kelley's report to the Knights. She mentioned nearly running into Andy. They got all over me about that until I explained that he wasn't supposed to be the delivery boy. The fact that he volunteered to deliver it to you without telling me raised a lot of red flags for the Knights. They've been working into the night on putting the pieces of the puzzle together. I got a call forty minutes ago to come here and fill you in on what we know. Andy's original link to the mob comes through his father's auto body shop. It's a regular chop shop, but the mob gets him to disassemble cars they don't want traced. Kinda hard to run down a car used in commission of a felony if the fenders are in Lake Forest and the carburetor's in Joliet. Andy used to manage that side of the business, before somebody got the bright idea to have him join the force."

"So removing an alternator and a battery would be a piece of cake for him."

"You know I just was thinking that very thought. Something else that just occurred to me. It woulda been hard to do it all alone in the dark on a cold night without anybody getting suspicious. It's a busy street. But if you got a tow truck parked next to your car..."

"Hide in plain sight. AAA to the rescue. Probably had Joey put the flashers on and everything."

"So Joey was sucked into this somehow," Tom said.

"They didn't know Joey was my guy until I called him. But they didn't want to wait until the dead of night again and needed the cover of a truck to avoid attention. They had to see Joey when I called him over. That means they're watching me."

"And I caught Joey in a lie."

"Yeah, but a complicated lie. A forced lie," I said, "Too complicated."

"How's that?"

"What did he tell you about me stiffing him?"

"Yeah. On a set of four tires."

"Not just tires, *Michelins*. Really? That's way too much tire for me and Joey knows it. The only reason to say it is to tip you off that his statement was queer. He also knew you could disprove what he said in ten seconds by looking at the bald set of

Walmart tires I got on there now. He was letting us know it's bullshit, without the people who sucked him in being able to figure it out."

"Are you able to forward messages from that thing?" he said, gesturing at my phone.

"For 650 bucks I better be."

"Forward both those messages to me and I'll take that back to the Knights, maybe it'll make them a little more comfortable about you."

"Why should they be uncomfortable about me?"

"Their man investigating an Italian mob connection in Chicago is named Cosmo Grande? You might be *their* dago, but you're still a dago, right? I'm not even sure how much they trust me, being a Chicago cop and all. They already know the kid is dirty. And you can bet your Bears tickets they did the same check on me that they did on him."

Tom sat back as if feeling more relaxed. He seemed to notice the bibles for the first time since sitting down.

"What about these? What have you figured—"

His phone rang abruptly and he raised an index finger in apology and took the call. A dark expression crossed his face.

"All right," he said. "Damn. I'm a couple minutes away. I'll fill you in on what happened here when I get there."

He hung up his phone and grabbed his coat as if forgetting I was in the room.

"What's up?" I said.

"Town Hall Station got a call ten minutes ago. Shots fired near the Belmont Harbor parking lot. They sent a squad car over and found Joey Greco in his tow truck, shot twice in the head."

"Double tap, mob style," I said.

"Guy that did it must have been sitting in the cab with him the whole time we talked."

CHAPTER FIFTEEN

saw Tom out the door and shook a tray of cubes into a water glass and filled it nearly to the brim from the fresh bottle of Jack. I had slept through the afternoon and evening and figured I was going to be up a while. I found a John Wayne marathon on cable and me and the Duke cleaned up the old west until three or four in the morning, when I finally fell asleep with the empty glass still balanced on my chest and no more idea of what I'd gotten myself into than a pit bull in a pinafore.

━━━

I was just waking up when the phone rang midmorning the next day.

"It's time to bring you completely up to speed," Don Bruster said when I answered.

"So are your shining Knights finally going to suffer a wop like me in the inner circle?" I was very much aware of the anger in my own voice, and made no effort to control it.

"Don't worry about them. Can I help it if some people still equate Chicago with the old outfit? So far no tommy guns, just one unfortunate civilian shot in the head. Know this, Cosmo, when I went to bat for you I laid my reputation on the line. That's looking like enough for them, at least for now. None of the Knights wants this case to blow us up and it has shown every potential for doing just that. I have the executive committee convinced that we don't have to pull the plug in Chicago just yet.

I hope I'm right. I need your help now more than ever. Trust me on that."

Don's composure in the face of the chaos that confronted us actually seemed to relax me. I made a bet with myself that he knew what he was doing after all.

"I'm calling from Midway Airport right now," he said. "I'm waiting for a package to be hand delivered by a Knight from out McTighue's way. Here's what I need you to do. I need to see you and I don't want whoever is keeping tabs on you to know about it. The Knights sent a cab for you. It should be in the alley out your back door. Make sure the driver has a deacon's cross on his lapel and look for something green. Could be a dab of paint or a ribbon or a Rolling Rock beer bottle, but something prominent, and green. Don't get in unless you see it. Nobody on the outside knows the color green is code."

"Where's the cab taking me?"

"The driver has been briefed. Ricobene's Restaurant on Pulaski, just southeast of the airport in a strip mall. I'll be waiting for you, with a big friggin gob of tomato sauce on my tie and a smile on my face."

He allowed himself a laugh and then hung up.

I walked to the back of the condo and peaked down at the alley. A yellow cab sat idling there, huffing a great plume of exhaust in the cold morning air. I dug my .38 out of the bureau, checked the five rounds, spun the empty chamber to the hammer position, and slipped the gun into my shoulder holster. I threw my coat on and shrugged at it so the rig was harder to see and went out to the waiting cab. The driver who rolled down his window at my approach was no larger than a circus bear and was wearing the deacon cross with a green felt background around it. I shook his thick hand and got in the back of the cab and he drove off without either of us speaking a word. The streets were frozen hard in places and the snow cracked beneath our tires as we wended our way south, into the heart of the city. My cell phone rang. I had a feeling who it might be, and was right. "So, Kelley, how has your morning been so far?"

"Better than that poor guy they found."

She was trying to sound upbeat but wasn't doing a very good job. It brought back memories of Peggy. I used to hear that same tension in her voice, especially near the end of our relationship, when she was trying to be nice to me and I was still trying to be Cosmo the Magnificent. I didn't know what to say to Kelley so I shut up.

"I heard you had a bomb scare too. Cosmo, are you okay?" The genuine concern I heard in her voice touched me.

"I'm fine, I think. But more confused than ever." I lowered my voice, even though I knew my driver was supposed to be one of the good guys. "I'm on my way to meet Don at Ricobene's. They sent a driver. I take it you heard about my car."

I looked out the window and saw that we were on Lake Shore Drive just before the turn onto the Stevenson Expressway past McCormick Place. The architectural monstrosity that is the new Soldier Field went by on the east side of the Drive. How Mayor Daley, "Richard the Younger" as Mike Royko used to call him, ever blessed its design—alien mother ship meets Roman Coliseum—is beyond imagining. I put us about twenty minutes from the restaurant, give or take an hour, depending on traffic, Chicago style.

I needed to get as much as I could out of Kelley, presuming she knew more than I did. At this juncture I had the feeling that just about everyone who wouldn't be sleeping under a Chicago bridge tonight knew more than me. I was starting to get angry, and decided to let her know it.

"This cloak and dagger crap is starting to piss me off. You and Don have got to start filling in some blanks." By then the expressway had jammed to a near halt and we weren't even at

Damen yet. My driver was hearing a lot more than I necessarily wanted him to. I said to Kelly, "How about if I shut up now and you start telling me what you're thinking is."

"I'm thinking that I really don't like the prospect of staying home all day. I'm going to tell my security detail that there might be some new evidence for me to check on back at the office. I'm guessing I really may find answers down there. Like how Andy is involved in this. Someone has drawn my boss and my ex-husband together in some kind of unholy alliance. I shudder to think who."

"We're on the same page. You may be onto something. Can it wait 'til I can join you?"

"I'll fill you in later."

"At least fill me in on your meeting yesterday." Almost like magic, the traffic that had been crawling was now up to speed and we were fast approaching the Pulaski exit. "Briefly. I'm getting close to the restaurant."

"I'll keep it short. There's not much to share anyway. The Knights understand now that Waterman's death has gotten them involved in something much deeper than some internal diocesan dust up. They aren't happy at being blindsided. These are men who value control above all else, and they don't have any here. Don kept trying to assure them that it will all work out and their cover won't be blown. But they may be on the cusp of a financial scandal that will rock the church to its foundation.

"Let me ask you about something that has been troubling me, though," she said. "Why would any of these players put the battery back into your car? It doesn't make sense."

"I got a theory. Why do you do anything, then do the opposite?"

She pondered a minute and said, "You changed your mind."

"Or you got a better idea. They slowed me down, and that could have been the end of it, but what if I tell the cops the battery and alternator were stolen but they end up not being missing at all. It's an attempt to discredit me."

"They phone in the bomb scare just to make sure you make that statement to the cops. That's really devious. It sounds so much like Andy."

"He wanted me to look like a feckless drunk who can't find his own butt with both hands and a flashlight."

"Actually you are doing a pretty good job of that yourself." I didn't have much to say to that. "Don sold you to the Knights as the best P.I. in Chicago. But, honestly, Cosmo, you're not cutting it. You insist on fogging your brain with weed and drowning yourself in booze. I can see how meeting me might have freaked you out and for that I guess I am partly to blame. I shouldn't have been so flippant about it. Mom loved you, and I care about you too. I don't want to see you messed up. But I can't let the Knights' cover be blown. And I don't want what's happening here to explode in the church's face. A lot of good people will be hurt. Not just the crooks. So forget your sad story about what happened to you forty years ago. For me..." Her voice got softer. "And, for Mom, stop getting high, okay? Focus. Trust Don. Let him use you as he needs to, okay?"

"Did you just say that Peggy loved me?"

"Oh, sweet Lord! Are you hearing what I am saying?"

"Yes I am, Kelley, I really am. Know this. I won't let you down. Or your mother." Kelley remained silent. "I will never do anything to hurt you. You have become very important to me. Meeting you was like a miracle in my life."

She chuckled.

"The miracle, Cosmo, is how you crack me up. But listen to me now. I'll never admit that I said this to you no matter who may ask. Don and Tom and I know why those specific pages were torn out of the bibles. But we need it to look like you came up with the solution all on your own. It'll be more convincing if you really do."

We pulled up in front of the restaurant and the driver, who seemed to be listening intently to my end of the conversation, stopped the car, got out, and opened the door for me.

"One last thing," she said. "This is important."

I said, "Wait a sec," to her and held up one finger in a "wait a minute" gesture to the tree trunk of a driver standing outside the car and pulled the door closed. "Go ahead."

"Somewhere in your conversation with Don make sure that you mention that you have found how the three torn pages connect. Each one references the very mysterious high priest that Abraham encountered."

"Melchisedek? A priest forever?"

"Give the spoiled priest a prize! You got it! I'm proud of you. Telling Don you discovered that all the torn pages reference Melchisedek should get him to fill you in on what it means. But it *has* to look like it's something you've come up with yourself, so he can justify bringing you further into the circle. Just promise me on Mom's grave that you'll never tell him that I was the one who let you onto it."

I hadn't realized how high this conversation was lifting me until her last words. Just the mention of Peggy's grave tore into me. I was having feelings I hadn't felt in decades. I couldn't even respond when she said, "Good bye, Cosmo, and good luck. I'll be praying for you," and hung up. I sat there in the back of the cab, all alone, with my cell phone in my ear, for I don't know how long.

The driver startled me with a rap on the window.

"You okay?" he said.

I nodded and opened the door.

"You need anything else from me?" he said.

I put the phone into my shirt pocket. "Not unless you are a priest forever." He frowned in puzzlement. I was feeling more than a little puzzled myself.

My wise ass answer to his question made me feel a twinge of guilt and brought me back to the present moment. He was, after all, one of us, that is, if I were one of us myself. I invited him to come in and join Don and me, but he politely declined.

"I'll wait here," he said, remaining every inch a professional.

"Can I at least have them bring out a sandwich and a Coke?"

"Thanks. I got called out early and missed breakfast. I guess it's not against the rules. Make mine a beef and sausage combo, wet, with sweet peppers, no fries, and a Diet Coke."

"You might not be a real Chicago cabbie, but you sure know how to eat like one."

CHAPTER SIXTEEN

The diner was blindingly bright with fluorescent lights and white tile. It was a welcome oasis from the gloom outside. It was easy to spot Don. He was halfway through a breaded steak sandwich that sat in a puddle of tomato sauce on his plate. He didn't catch my coming in. He was looking down and rubbing his shirt vigorously with a napkin that he kept dipping into his water glass. Pink, damp stains were clearly visible on both his shirt and his tie.

"Hell, Don, you couldn't wait to order until I got here?" I said, standing right over him

He stopped working on the stains and looked towards me for the first time, totally unruffled. "Mel texted to say the two of you were running late. It smells so great in here I confess I succumbed to the temptation to start without you."

"Mel? That's the driver's name? You've got to be kidding."

There was a twinkle in his eye that pissed me off. I was determined not to ask if "Mel" was short for "Melchisedek."

"Waiter," Don called.

The waiter came right over. His name tag read "Ric." In fact, everyone who worked at the restaurant had a name tag that said "Ric." It was part of their image. Names were starting to bug me. I felt like I did after a peyote flashback nearly killed me one day when I decided to stroll down for a wade in the Pacific, not realizing Highway One lay between me and the beach.

"I'll have what my friend here is having but I promise not to dribble it on my shirt. I'll have a Coke too. And while you're at it, a combo, wet, with sweet peppers, and a Diet Coke to go for the guy in the yellow cab waiting outside. 'Mel' I think his name is."

Don smiled approvingly at my generosity towards Mel.

"Hot peppers on yours, just like Mr. Bruster?" the waiter said.

"Yeah, but how about onion rings instead if fries." The smells of the place, not least among them the aroma of fried onions, were beginning to make me salivate.

"That'll be right up," he said.

"It's past time to clue me in on what's going on," I said to Don when the waiter left. "Now there are two dead people in my life and I've got *ziti* to go on: your secret group of deacons, a couple of very weird break-ins, a car that has been dismantled and re-built, not one but two bomb threats, and three bibles, each with a page torn out. What is going on?"

Without looking up from his shirt, he just said, "You tell me."

I decided that I had nothing to lose by taking Kelley's advice. So I dove right in. "I've figured out what all three bibles have in common."

Don looked up at that. He put down the wet napkin and reached for his sandwich. His judge-like expression seemed geared to let me know that he was decidedly unimpressed. "Tell me what you found." With that he took another bite from his sandwich and I watched red sauce dribble onto the exact spot on the tie he had just cleaned. I will confess the darker angels of my nature enjoyed watching it splatter.

"All three torn pages reference the same person."

"Oh yeah? And who might that be?" His look was dutifully incredulous.

"I found that each of the torn pages has a reference to the high priest Melchisedek. You know, 'You are a priest forever...'"

"I'm familiar with the passages. What do you think it means? And how does it connect to Waterman?"

Unfortunately Kelley's tutorial on the phone had not gotten as far as making a connection. When you don't have the cards, bluff.

"I have my own theory on it, but I'd like to hear your take. You guys owe me whatever you've got after the way you have treated me so far."

Ric arrived with my food, giving us both a minute to consider what I'd said. The sandwich looked as great as it smelled. "This, my dear deacon, is how you wrestle a fried steak sandwich into submission, Chicago style." I picked it up with both hands, stuck my elbows out parallel to the table, leaned forward and took a generous bite. Peppers squirted out and thin slices of breaded beefsteak covered in tomato sauce fell harmlessly onto my plate and nowhere near my shirt front.

While Don did his laundry I bit into a perfect onion ring. It was crisp on the outside and wet and soft on the inside. The onion was sweet and cooked just right so that you could bite through it and leave the rest in the coating. Don finally gave the tie a few last swipes and rinsed his fingers in his water glass.

I took another bite from my sandwich. An intense blast of heat from the hot giardiniera sent me diving to my glass of Coke for relief. It was an incredible blend of flavors and textures.

"Cosmo, you are a dear friend. When I told you early on that you have to trust me I had no idea things could unfold the way they have."

While I chewed I entertained a notion to ease off on Don a little. He is a friend. But I just couldn't help myself. My gut kept reminding me that when something starts to make a guy squirm, let him squirm. I stuck my finger in the wound and gave it a little jab.

"Unfold? That's kind. More like unravel."

But Don didn't get to be one of the toughest judges in Cook County for nothing. He laughed me off. Then he wiped the sauce on his plate with the last of the bread from his sandwich, still not about to show me his hand. He called one of the Rics over to our table. "Two cannolis, filled fresh please, and two coffees."

I added, "How about making that that three and sending one of each out to the cab." I hoped that Mel had enjoyed his sandwich. I really needed to ask him if that was his real name.

"I stand corrected," Don said with grace, "make it three." He waited expectantly until Ric was out of earshot and said, "I may be rushing things, but I need to tell you about the package from Tulsa."

I had become so consumed in the cat and mouse, not to mention steak giardiniera and onion rings, that I had forgotten why we were meeting so close to the airport. I figured that I was about to be handed another disconnected piece of an ever-expanding puzzle. I pushed myself back from the table. My plate was empty. A different Ric cleared the table. Don waited until the cannolis and coffee arrived and we were alone once more before he began talking, at which point he leaned forward.

"What I have is a six-inch file on your old friend Bishop McTighue's financial dealings back from the time he joined the seminary faculty, through his stint as an auxiliary bishop, all the way through his getting his own diocese in Tulsa. One of our guys there, a deacon, used to work for the IRS."

I interrupted with a laugh. "Isn't working for the Feds an impediment to Holy Orders?"

"Should be. But when our guy saw what disregard the bishop had for financial accountability and transparency, he began to check out the money McTighue was spending outside the diocese on condos in Puerto Rico, Florida, the Turks and Caicos, New York, and right here in the Windy City. He uses a lot of shadow companies, but we are putting together some pretty damning stuff. It's all here."

"So, what's so earthshaking about all that? Bishops have been free spenders since Paul bribed Peter at the First Council of Jerusalem. Anything to stop him from keeping the religion kosher. Why such great concern among you Knights about this guy?"

"It's not all that clean. A lot of the investments are quite troubling. A few hotels, maybe black hotels, not even all stateside."

"Black hotels?"

"Yeah. You want to launder dirty money, you build a luxury hotel. You never have to turn on the lights, hence 'black,' but you claim you fill it up every night with a bunch of high-rollers and their girlfriends who prefer to pay cash. Couple hundred rooms, couple thousand a night for every suite."

"I'm in the wrong business."

"I hear what you're saying. A lot of it looks like business-as-usual. And a lot of it is hidden deep in layers of shadow companies. But given the climate and the people's anger with the church, we thought it best if we could simply get the old bugger to retire early and fade into the sunset before the *Sun-Times* gets hold of it. That's what got us started."

"And how were you planning on getting him to retire?"

"We were ready to move on him when Waterman decided on his own to bring him down personally. That stopped us in our tracks, especially after we heard that Waterman had contacted you. Before we were able to straighten things out, he's dead in his condo. We couldn't have expected that. Our plans have fallen apart and we find ourselves scrambling to keep up. No offense, good friend, but you were not a part of our plans. But we adapted. We figured, frankly, that we'd use your independent investigation, about which we enjoy complete deniability, to frighten McTighue. But before we even began to adjust we find ourselves visited by murder, bomb threats, and chaos. We don't know who is doing what or why." Don leaned forward and lowered his voice. "I have, in this case, hard evidence that McTighue has crossed his syndicate partners. Evidently they have it in for him as much as we do. Would I mind if some kind of 'accident' befell him? I won't answer that. But if any of what's in here becomes public, it could bring the church in Chicago to its knees, and not in prayer. I refuse to let that happen on my watch. It would bring down a lot of the good guys, the Knights and all those we've got working with us, people like Tom and Kelley and even you. So there will be no more hiding anything from you. I've made that executive decision. All of us, including you, me, Tom, and Kelley are going to meet at the Cardinal Stritch Retreat House on the campus of Mundelein Seminary tonight at 8:00 p.m. One of our people is in charge. And there happens to be a retreat for deacons going on there right now. Coincidentally," he said with a flicker of his eyebrows, "they all happen to be either on our board or vetted field agents like Mel. Imagine that. They are the brain trust and we will have one night with them to figure out what we have to do, and do soon, and do right. We expect that we're only going to get one shot at it."

"That's all fine and good," I said. "But why do you still need me if all your original plans have fallen apart. I'm not one of you, remember? You don't see any green on my lapel, do you?"

"That's exactly why we need you. You aren't a Knight. You have no history with us. So even if things get screwed up and the wrong people find out about you, they will have trouble tracing your actions back to us."

"So I'm nothing but a smokescreen."

"I understand what you are feeling, Cosmo. But to be honest, you no longer have a choice. Like it or not, you are in this too deep yourself. I am sorry now that I got you into this mess, but in it to your chinny chin chin you are. I promise I will make it up to you. You have my word. Now, Mel will drive you home. Pack an overnight bag and he'll get you up to Mundelein. For what it's worth, the cardinal is totally out of the loop on all this and that is where we intend to keep him. It's better that he concentrate on the really important stuff like whether priests are wearing the right color vestments every Sunday."

"What about Billy Gallo?"

"That's a tale we'll tell later tonight." The bible passages never came up again. Don got up and paid the check on his way out to a cashier whose name tag said "Ric."

CHAPTER SEVENTEEN

I kept my eyes closed most of the cab ride home. I was beginning to dread my choice of hot peppers with the sandwich. Mel was grateful for all the food sent out to him and told me how good it had been, but never spoke a word as he drove. I've had better conversations with a light post I found myself hanging onto for support. Traffic opened up and we were making good time. I wondered whether Mel was just respecting my need for quiet right now, or had been instructed to keep silent. I mulled over everything that Don had just said to me. A part of me was very angry at being used. And part of me was embarrassed. Had I really grown that inept? But at that moment I didn't have the luxury of feeling sorry for myself. Mel got me home in forty minutes.

He turned in the driver's seat without climbing out and opening the door and said, "I'll wait here. My instructions are to get you to Mundelein stat. Weather north of the city is a bear."

"Okay. I have to feed the cats, take a quick shower, and pack a bag. How's fifteen minutes?"

He nodded.

"You don't need to use the facilities?"

"Took care of that after the cannoli. Anyways, I figure safer to stay here and watch my cab so that nobody steals the carburetor."

He laughed, I didn't. What else did he know? That got me started all over again. He seemed to sense that his joke misfired and said, "I'll just stay here and keep the car warm," almost apologetically.

The condo, with no windows opened in weeks, smelled like a Grateful Dead jam at the lion house. No time to fix that. Under other circumstances I might have been tempted to smoke one joint for the road. But not today. I needed to be able to think clearly, something I was beginning to realize that I hadn't been doing a lot of lately. The cats ignored me even after I fed them and refilled their water bowl, their way of letting me know the litter boxes needed attention. But there was no time.

I hit the shower and mulled some more. It was no surprise to me that I didn't have a clue about what was going to happen at the summit at Mundelein. These guys had made a habit of keeping me in the dark. Still, after a few minutes under the hot water I realized why I was feeling anxious. I had not set foot on seminary property since I was kicked out in 1976. I had even avoided driving down Route 176 for all these years. Now I'm going up to the retreat house there with no time to sit and process my feelings. Cosmo, how do you get yourself into messes like this?

I dried myself off with the shirt I had just taken off and sniffed the clothes thrown around in my closet until I found some things to wear that fit the austerity of the occasion and didn't smell like wet sheep. I tossed some toiletries into an old duffle bag with fresh underwear and went back out to the cab.

The expression on Mel's face told me something was up.

"You didn't have your TV on did you?"

"What happened now?"

"There's a report of a big fire at Clark and Diversey."

"My office."

I thought about all that cash Waterman had given me and how I decided to stash it at home. Then I thought, with a sudden squirt of adrenalin, of old Levinson and Cashman, my neighbors. I felt a sharp twinge of guilt that they didn't come to mind first.

"I got to go there now."

Mel took a step towards me. "Sorry, man. No way. My instructions are to get you to the retreat house as quickly as I can. So that's where we're going. There's nothing you can do at your office anyways. It's too late to be a hero."

My car keys were on the dresser upstairs. Would my car even start? Might there be some evidence in it that my driving might destroy.

Mel stepped forward and blocked my path back to the condo to make sure I understood he'd use whatever force was necessary to make me follow his instructions from the Knights. He had about four inches and twenty pounds on me, and the twenty pounds did not include among them one ounce of doubt that I would come along to Mundelein quietly.

Now even a disciplined student of Tae Kwon Do like yours truly understands that a street fight is a completely different breed of cat from dancing around the dojo with a sparring partner in his pajamas. The guiding principal in a street fight is to hit a soft part of the other guy's body with a hard part of yours, or a hard part of his body with something even harder: a blackjack, a brick, a bag of hammers...anything at hand. It doesn't matter. Just not your fist. Breaking your hand on an opponent's clenched jaw is a sorrowful way to start a brawl. An elbow strike to the throat works great if you don't mind using lethal force, but usually I am just trying to get some huckleberry to stop annoying me. The solar plexus is my favorite target, a radiating bundle of nerves, the docs call it a rete, just below the sternum, where the chest meets the belly. It is a little below the eye line, so usually undefended. A proper strike starts all those nerves in a frenzy of random firing, fierce enough to cause the diaphragm to spasm, keeping the victim from even drawing a breath for a few long moments. Good technique requires that you lift your fingers back, relaxed, just to get them out of the way, and then drive the base of your palm like the tip of a lance, not at, but *through* the middle of the chest to an aim point eight inches behind it, not swinging from your elbow, or even your shoulder, but driving from the balls of your feet, transferring every pound of your body weight right through your target. Many who have received such a well-placed strike have been sure they were about to die, but most end up on their feet and walking around a few minutes later, shaking it off. So a palm strike to the solar plexus is my go-to in most threatening situations.

I used it on this deadbeat dad once not long ago, Buzz Walcsak, a steel-hauler from Merrillville who owned a fleet of forty trucks but found the support of his four children living in Emerson to be something of a nuisance. He called the butler inside and came out under his white-columned carriage porch brandishing a Colt .45 Buntline Special with a twelve-inch barrel. It was just the weapon Yosemite Sam, to whom Buzz, without the drooping moustache, bore a passing resemblance, would have chosen for the job. It was Buzz's misfortune that I knew the replica to be authentic, right down to its single-action firing mechanism, meaning you needed to pull the hammer back with your thumb before you could fire. Which Buzz had neglected to do. He might as well have been waving a smoked Vienna sausage in my face. A minute later he was lying in a bed of blue-ribbon begonias without enough wind in him to cry "Mama," and I was walking away with the fat wad of fifties he liked to flash bulging in my front pocket instead of his. Limping away, actually, with the barrel end of the Buntline in my waistband biting wickedly at my thigh.

So Mel stood in front of me now with his hands on his hips, blocking my path. He might as well have stripped to the waist and painted a big red bull's eye on his belly.

"You're forgetting just one thing," I said.

"What?"

I pointed straight up in the air with my left hand and when his glance turned up I let him have it.

I jumped into the running cab and drove off a few seconds later with Mel on all fours vomiting chunks of the finest beef and sausage combo in the known universe—wet, with sweet peppers, no fries—into the snow around him.

I felt my head start to clear and got that sudden whoosh of adrenaline that follows any combat, however sure the outcome. My only real concern now was those two neighbors on either side of my office. I didn't want them to become innocent victims of a mess of my creation. I needed to know that they were safe. They had to be. Damn Waterman. Damn McTighue. Damn Don and the Knights. Damn Gallo. Damn me.

Fire equipment, emergency vehicles, and TV vans blocked Clark, Diversey, and Broadway. I whipped the cab into the Century Mall parking garage, marveling at how wide a path other vehicles gave to a careering Chicago cab. Might have to make it my next vehicle of choice.

I took the stairs down the nearly deserted mall two at a time, burst onto Clark and sprinted south past Jamba Juice. No one tried to stop me as I ducked between firemen, police officers, and television film crews. I slowed down as I noticed that the fire hoses were being rolled back up and some of the engines were leaving. The building was still standing, looking not so much the worse for the wear. There were a couple of broken windows, but the walls weren't frosted with ice from the hoses.

To my enormous relief I picked out Levinson and Cashman standing so close to each other that their hands touched. When I stepped into their view they both turned my way smiling. Smiling? But then, who doesn't love the entertainment value of a minor catastrophe.

"What happened?"

Levinson was more breathless than usual. "That cop over there told me that some kind of incendiary device was left on the loading dock."

I must have looked confused. Cashman decided to clarify it for me.

"A friggin bomb, that's what it was," she said. "But most of the propellant didn't ignite. Me and Levinson & Son here would be ashes in the wind if it had. You know what I mean?" She reached into her pocket and handed me a comb that glows in the dark. "Comb your hair, Cosmo. You look like you just rolled out of bed."

"I was afraid it was some kind of three-alarm pull and the building was destroyed."

Levinson shook his head. "Probably some media putz pumping the story. Just a couple of guys with cameras showed up. They're packing up already. A small bomb in an old building doesn't make the headlines these days." He almost seemed disappointed. "Look. They're taking down the yellow tape. They told us that's when we could go back in."

They started forward with some of the other tenants, leaving me alone and confused. I noticed that the lights in the shoe store on the ground level were on. The power hadn't even gone out. My phone rang. Of course it was Don. I braced for an ear-beating about hitting Mel, my little act of grand theft auto, and, last if not least, about blowing off his big summit.

Instead I heard, "Hey! Mike Tyson. Why are you going around slugging peace-loving deacons? I just got a call from Mel, who, by the way, is breathing again."

"No apology from me on that one, Donny Boy. He told me that my office building was burning down. I'm standing here looking at it and am guessing I won't even have any water damage. So what's up with him? I'm getting damned tired of being the last guy in line to hear what the hell is going on."

"It's just as well things turned out like they did. Tom showed up with the bomb squad to check your car again about the time Mel got his wind back. If you'd have tried to take your car to your office you'd have been blown into Belmont Harbor."

"Whiskey Tango Foxtrot!"

"Someone wanted you to start your car in a hurry, not thinking about what the consequences might be. The bomb at your office was a decoy, a trap to send you running to the car."

"Why do you say that with such confidence?"

"I spoke to Tom. The bomb only partially detonated. That's pretty unusual. If these are the people we think they are, they've had plenty of practice. It was designed to be a dud, or Clark Street would look like downtown Baghdad right now. You still need to get in there and see if anything is disturbed or missing. Was there anything in your office tying you to the Knights?"

"Not a thing. You haven't mentioned Kelley. How is she?"

"She's sitting here next to me in the retreat director's suite. She's a little worried about you. But she's safe as she can be here. We've checked. Her condo is untouched. She did get a call from Gallo wanting her at her desk tomorrow."

"You're not going to let her go in, are you?"

"I can't really give you an answer to that. Sometime tonight we'll figure what's best."

"Am I still supposed to join you up there?"

"No hurry. I like you right where you are. Take your time. Remember, I trust you. Find something out that will be helpful. After you're done there, I'm pretty sure that it will be safe for you to go home. Mel has secured your condo and is keeping an eye on the car now. Be nice to him. He was just doing his job."

"And just how did he get in?"

"Remember the friendly and helpful locksmith from AAA who left your new keys at the bar?"

"Don't tell me. A Knight of St. Thomas operative. So everyone south of Waukegan has a key to my place. You are a bastard."

I wanted to be angry, but Don's belly laugh at the other end took the wind out of my sails. I just hung up and walked up to my office. Levinson was bent to his work and Cashman's door was closed. Business as usual. My own door was jimmied and ajar. I pulled out my gun. The light was on. The room had been tossed, but whoever did it was gone. It's not exactly the Library of Congress, so it didn't take me long to make sure that nothing was missing. Half the files were on the floor, half were left alone, as if someone had found just what they had come looking for. But they were nothing but old case files I should have purged years ago. I sat down and cleared my mind as best I could, with a longing glance towards the T-is-for-Tennessee-whiskey file drawer.

Whoever did this wasn't fooling me. The bomb got me pointed here all right, just not in the car they wanted me to blow up in. The rest of the show was a red herring, not for me, but for the men they figured would be investigating my untimely death. If the bad guys had succeeded in blowing me up, the undisguised break-in at into my office would falsely suggest some guilty evidence had been found. Why do you stop tossing an office halfway through your search unless you found what you were looking for? If the cops tried to pursue the non-existent trail of evidence from the break-in, the whole thing would have been cold cased in a month.

Everything had been set up perfectly. It was the old Chicago outfit at its elegant best. Perpetuate the myth that they're just a bunch of dumb brutes punching ice picks in people's ears. The dumber they let themselves look, the easier for them to succeed. So they make sure that the bomb doesn't touch my office, or do much damage for that matter, even though they want it to look like they were out to blow it all up. But who the hell are *they?* And why are they coming after me with such a studied vengeance? I had no answers. But I knew just the guy who might. I looked up a number I had not referred to for at least ten years and got the appointment I wanted with a single call, as I knew I would.

CHAPTER EIGHTEEN

I t took me the afternoon to clean up my office. I took small comfort in reassembling the scattered dead investigation files, every one of them small beer. The way I work, most of them just contained a contract and an invoice. When I had everything in order, and assured myself once again that nothing was missing, I shut off the lights and used a key to turn the deadbolt on the door, which I had neglected to do the last time I left. It's why it had been so easy for my intruder to jimmy the door. I should have known better. Shame on me for being so careless. Like I said earlier, I've found myself slipping lately. I walked quickly back to the cab in the parking garage with my hands stuffed into my pockets. The evening had turned bitter cold without a cloud in the sky and the stars themselves seemed to shiver in the night air. Late winter had the city and me in its unrelenting grip. I knew I had to get home, warm up, and find a way to sort everything out.

Still, I was in no hurry to face Mel, however well he may have recovered from the blow. The physical pain had surely passed, but the humiliation of getting suckered might remain. So I took Broadway and stopped at Treasure Island to get us both something to eat, kind of a peace offering on my part. I went to the deli counter and filled my cart with fresh sliced prosciutto, pistachio mortadella, sopressata, and genoa salami—all the fixings for a killer sandwich. I found some nice aged provolone cheese to finish it off and grabbed a crusty loaf of Italian bread, dusted with flour and still warm from the oven. Then I picked out some nice, firm plum tomatoes, probably shipped from Chile this time of year. And I added a jar of sweet giardiniera to the rest of the fixings in my cart. I had my fill of the hotter version at lunch. I thought that the fresh baked lemon meringue pie I set in the cart was going to be the last item until I found a cooler full of Pabst Blue Ribbon six packs. Thanks to the benevolence of the beer gods it's being brewed again and it tastes just like it used to, like real beer. As a steelworker I knew in my youth once told me, "I like a beer that bites back." Ironic that the North Side yuppies have embraced the beer I grew up on, calling it PBR. The bill for it all ran to nearly one hundred dollars and the stuff barely filled two shopping bags. Thanks to the late Ed Waterman, God rest his soul, I didn't have to worry about that.

I took side streets the rest of the way home. Most folks were in for the night, their house lights blazing, warm and snug with their families. Winter loneliness was starting to roll over me. Cars were parked at varying angles against the curb to avoid ruts in the crusted snow or just left askew because they were stuck. I found a spot in front of a barely visible fire hydrant close to my building and parked the faux cab there. I did allow myself a glimmer of a smile at the thought that it might be ticketed or towed. My frustrations at how I had been treated, and my puzzlement over what was happening to me, were morphing into anger again.

When I got to my front door I heard voices inside. Mel must have made himself at home in front of my TV. I turned the unlocked knob. The TV wasn't on. I walked in to find Mel and Tom listening to a very animated Don. Kelley was there too, with her legs folded on the chair that seemed to have become her seat of choice. An open, extra-large pizza box from Leona's was on the coffee table. Except for a few crusts, it was empty. Six dead bottles of Miller Lite were scattered around the room. Don stopped talking when I walked in, and they all turned as if on cue and looked at me.

"I'm sorry I missed the party." And looking down at the empty box, "Thanks for saving me some leftovers." I got a warm and cozy feeling about where I parked the cab.

Don spoke first. "Was anything taken from your office? We heard it was trashed."

"How could you possibly know that? Let me guess. One of the firemen at the scene is one of your friggin good guys, right? And what the hell are you all doing here?"

"Actually, it's the department chaplain. And, yes, he did report back to us. You got it. Congratulations on your new-found powers of deduction." Don clapped his hands together and was quickly joined by the others in mock applause. "Kelley and I left the retreat house and called Tom to meet us here. Mel ordered the pizza. It's time for you to get on the same page as the rest of us."

"Same page? We're not even reading the same book."

Kelley laughed again. Before she could say that I crack her up, I shot her the look I used to give her mother when she pissed me off. It usually succeeded in shutting Peggy up and it had the same effect on her daughter now. I was sore tired of being the butt of their jokes, and wanted them all to know it. Friends are not supposed to make friends look foolish.

"I'm surrounded by people who keep telling me half-truths. And you are expecting me to figure out a murder while I'm dodging bombs that aren't there but then appear and bombs that are set but don't go off, not to mention multiple break-ins, and oh yah, my dead friend Joey, who did nothing worse than try to help me out of a jam."

"I guess it's time to fess up, Don." Tom didn't look up at either me or Don as he spoke. He just studied the label on the beer bottle in his hands. I remembered how much he hated light beers. "The poor guy has a right to know."

"Fess up to what?"

"Tom's right," Mel piped in. "Merciful God, the poor slob will never be able to figure it out all by himself."

I looked over at Mel. "How's the solar plexus, buddy? Hurts, don't it?" Now it was my turn to laugh. Nobody else joined in. I stopped and looked at the other three. I felt an irrepressible need to assume control. "No one is telling me anything until I make myself a sandwich." I carried the bags into the kitchen without waiting for a reply.

Kelley followed me. "Cosmo, stop being such a hard ass. Go out there and listen. I'll make your freaking sandwich. There's a lot to talk about." She left me no real choice, giving me the same half-pleading, half-challenging look her mother always used to wear me down.

I threw up my arms in mock surrender and grabbed one of the six packs of Pabst out of the bag. I'd been behaving myself far too well, and suddenly I was very thirsty.

"I'm back and I'm all ears," I said, walking into the living room.

Don rubbed his hands together in a strange mix of glee and getting down to the task at hand. "First of all, Cosmo, there were not two murders. Waterman's death was most definitely a suicide. We have known that all along. But we thought we could use the doubts about his death to our advantage. I know that doesn't sound very nice, but…" He shrugged his shoulders.

"Machiavellian," I said, in mock condemnation. I shot a quick look at Tom, who had been playing me all along. He shrugged and continued the careful scrutiny of the label on his beer bottle.

I chugged a Pabst. While everyone seemed to be waiting for my reaction to what Don had just said, Kelley had walked in from the kitchen and tossed my sandwich on top of the pizza box.

"So *all* of you knew that Waterman committed suicide?" They all nodded in silent agreement, even Mel. "So why did you think you had to keep me in the dark?" I reached down, grabbed the sandwich with my free hand, and took a hearty bite. The prosciutto was sliced thin as a butterfly wing, and the shaved mortadella melted like butter in my mouth. The provolone was nutty and dry and a perfect complement to the salty meats and the peppery bite of the sopressata. I washed it down with the beer, wishing I had a glass of Chianti instead.

""Cosmo," Don looked almost apologetic, "we brought you on board because we thought it would look better if an outsider deciphered what would appear to be a message from the dead, so to speak. McTighue suspects our existence, so we had to stay in the shadows. We needed a disinterested third party to put the fear of God into him, the fear that Waterman's death was going to be investigated as a murder."

"So you never brought me in to investigate anything. I was nothing more than your stalking horse."

He started again but this time more slowly. "The Knights first caught onto McTighue because of some shady land deals he was involved in with property in Bridgeview. That's all. It's just like I told you. Unfortunately, at the same time, Waterman was getting increasingly ticked off about not being allowed back as a priest after his wife died. It should have been a simple matter, as you know, because he had never been officially laicized by Rome. But McTighue held some old grudges and threw a wrench in the works, all the way from Tulsa. That self-righteous bastard convinced the cardinal that it would be a scandal to let Waterman back in, despite the precedents. Meanwhile McTighue is sitting on his own very real scandal, one that could bring financial ruin to the archdiocese here and even domino across the country."

"Why don't you just confront the bastard yourselves, or take your information directly to the cardinal or even to Rome?"

"That would have blown our cover once and for all. We are working on other highly delicate situations around the country that we don't want to jeopardize. We have to stay below the radar if we are going to be effective. Besides, McTighue would claim that we are just a bunch of liberal malcontents out to malign a loyal servant of Holy Mother Church. We found ourselves getting into something bigger than anyone expected. We needed to step back, watch as things unfolded, and improvise where needed. Obviously, Joey's death, the phone threats, the bombs, these things are telling us that there are players out there that don't want to be drawn into what we are discovering."

"And who might those players be?"

"Like I said at the restaurant, we are firmly convinced that Bishop McTighue is entangled with organized crime. But I'm mightily confused at how thoroughly they've been botching up what they are trying to do."

"And what might it be that they are trying to do?" I downed half of my second Pabst and decided to stop there, following Kelley's earlier advice.

Don just shrugged his shoulders and laughed. "That's what we are trying to figure out."

I looked over at Tom, who had remained quiet. "What do you think?"

"I know for certain that Waterman did commit suicide. My buddies in forensics say so. He even left a note that no one outside this room or the Knight's council knows about. He missed his wife. With his hopes dashed about returning to the priesthood he had nothing left to live for but to try to get even with McTighue. Waterman talked to me before he met with you. That was when I brought the Knights in. He had already been to see Billy Gallo with information he had garnered himself about the shady land deals, maybe more. But it appears that the good chancellor chose to ignore it. Don has gotten additional information from sources in Tulsa that prove Waterman's allegations. But it's all veiled by dummy corporations, and bank failures, the kind of stuff that could keep a prosecutor, if you got one interested, tied up for years."

Mel chimed in. "So Waterman brings in a neutral, but according to Don, a trustworthy private eye who, after reviewing a little doctored evidence, would create a reasonable suspicion that his death was a murder. We could take that information to McTighue and scare him into retiring. We thought that he would never admit outright to any fraudulent land dealings, and he has been pretty good at covering his trail. But we figured that knowing he might be implicated in a highly publicized murder would convince him to disappear for good. Not a totally satisfying conclusion, maybe not justice, but enough for us."

Don said, "Cosmo, we were never as clear about McTighue's ties with the mob as we are now. No one has the nerve to tangle directly with them. So our plans have radically changed. No more using you. We are asking for your help. This time as an investigator, not a stalking horse. What do you say?"

I finished the last bite of my sandwich while thinking about my theory on the defective bomb and the routing, not searching, of my office. But after being kept in the dark myself, I didn't mind letting them swing in the breeze a while. I had questions, not answers.

"Before we go any farther, Don, why don't you explain why you tore the pages out of the three bibles."

CHAPTER NINETEEN

Before Don could answer, my cell phone rang. The caller's name was blocked. Those are the kind of calls I typically ignore. But there was nothing typical about today, so with one hand I put my finger to my lips to quiet everyone in the living room. I pressed SPKR PHN and then answered with a simple "Hello."

"Grande." We could all recognize the ever-melodious voice of Billy Gallo. Things were getting even more interesting. "Gallo here. Listen, I need to talk to you in my office, 8:00 a.m. sharp tomorrow morning and not a minute earlier or a minute later. Got it?"

I looked around the room to get some kind of consensus as to how to respond. Don already was nodding up and down like a bobble-head doll in the back window of a low rider, mouthing "yes" over and over again. The rest, while less excited than Don, seemed in agreement with him.

Despite Don's earlier promises to clarify everything, I was still feeling pushed around and decided to push back.

"Depends, Gallo. I'm awfully busy right now. What is it that you want so desperately to talk to me about?"

Don nodded his head even more vigorously in approval at what I said and began rubbing his hands together in that weird sort of way of his. His juices were flowing. This was the kind of repartee he enjoyed.

Gallo didn't miss a beat. "Busy doing what? Cleaning up the mess from your bombing?"

I raised an eyebrow at his comment. The fire had been on the news, briefly, but the cause was only reported as "under investigation." I wasn't sure whether he really had an inside track and used the word "bombing" to impress me or whether he was fishing for a reaction. So I ignored it.

"I'm guessing it has something to do with Waterman."

"Yeah, Cosmo, you're right. Aren't you always right? Just be on time. I'll be at the main entrance waiting to let you in. Don't even ring the bell. And, by the way, it was a good idea to remember to deadbolt the door of your office when you left today." He hung up without waiting for a reaction.

"That was an interesting little twist at the end," Tom said. "He's got people checking up on you, Cosmo. But tell me, does anyone here doubt he's up to his elbows in this?" Head shakes around the room. "Anyone want to venture a guess how?"

Kelley, who had remained uncharacteristically quiet, surprised us all by being the first to break the silence. "Jesus! A judge, a cop, a P.I., and a...?" She paused not knowing exactly what to call Mel. So I helped her by chiming in with..."a hack." He shot me a sour look and she continued. "None of you can see it, can you?"

"See what?" I said, with mounting frustration. "If you think you know something, spit it out, girl."

"We suspect that McTighue is in deep with the mob. We also have long suspected that Gallo has some kind of connections to them as well. Something or, to my point, *someone* ties Gallo, the mafia, Waterman, the police investigation, and, unless I miss my guess, McTighue together. Can't any of you see it? It's so obvious. Who is the one person connected to all those threads of the spider web? We looked at each other silently, in puzzlement, until Tom let out a groan.

"How did I not see it? Right in front of my nose."

"It's Andy," Kelley said. "My ex-husband, your partner. Cosmo's messenger, Gallo's son-in-law, with decades-old ties to the mob through his father's chop shop."

She stared at us triumphantly before settling back onto the chair, curling her leg under her in the process.

"He probably stuck around and watched you after delivering the bible I sent," Tom said. "Decided to slow you down. Disabled your car. Then he got a better idea."

Mel said, "You're not suggesting…"

"Ballistics show Joey Greco was shot at close range with a .38. With a light load."

"A cop's gun," I said.

"Not your main weapon, these days. But the kind you keep strapped to your ankle. The kind Andy kept strapped to his ankle."

"I bet it isn't strapped there now," I said.

Don turned to Tom. "How much does the kid know about what really happened to Waterman and how much might he know about us?"

"I think we're okay. I don't think he knows anything about the Knights. He still thinks we're dealing with a homicide, which is fine with me. He probably suspects I cut Cosmo some slack as a person of interest because we go back the way we do. But thinking about it, he does ask a lot of questions."

"He's somebody's boy. But whose?" Mel asked. "Is he in Gallo's pocket or the mob's?" We sat in quiet contemplation of that puzzle.

"No," Kelley said. "He's not *somebody's* boy. He's *everybody's* boy. That is, everybody thinks he is *their* inside guy. Like a double agent."

"Maybe triple," I said. "There's no love lost between Gallo and McTighue. The outfit thinks they own him and think he is giving them the inside scoop on Gallo and McTighue."

"And the same goes for Gallo and McTighue," Tom said. "Everybody trusts Andy."

"And everybody is getting screwed by Andy," Kelley said. "He's got three tigers by the tail if this thing blows up."

"Gives him some serious skins in the game," Tom said.

"So how do I play that when I meet with Gallo tomorrow?" I said.

"For starters, let me fill in some more of the blanks for you," Don said. "I was the one who tore the pages out of the bibles. It broke my heart to desecrate Waterman's. AAA Locksmiths got me into your place to get your bible. Kelley needed some convincing before she let me tear the page out of hers. And, by the way, no one ever broke into her place. We staged that to build our legend."

"Here's what you were supposed to figure out about the Melchisedek connection. McTighue's episcopal crest reads 'You are a priest forever.' Now, if you would, please tell me, where were the three bibles resting when you first saw them?"

"Waterman's was on the footrest next to his bed."

"How about yours?"

"Right over there." I pointed to my ottoman. "You're telling me that you took it off the bookshelf, ripped out a page, and put it there on purpose?"

He ignored my question. "And where did Kelley tell you hers was left?"

"Something about a stool or ottoman as well."

"And what's another name for an ottoman or a footrest? How about 'footstool'? Now does that tell you anything?"

"'You are a priest forever,'" I quoted from memory from the pages of the Psalms torn from my bible, "'according to the order of Melchisedek, and I will make your enemies your footstool.' You wanted me to make a connection between Waterman and McTighue, a message from the dead just before he was murdered so I could pin it on McTighue. But what about the threats on the computers and the hanging and drowned stuffed cats?"

"You weren't getting it, Cosmo," Don said.

"You kept getting your head stuck up a bottle of Jack," Kelley said, not kindly.

"We had to keep pressing," Don said. "We needed you to create an apparently independent case that Waterman had been murdered in a conspiracy involving McTighue, and make a strong enough case to scare him out of his wits. To make him vulnerable to pressure to resign. We want him to go quietly, not to blow the Knights across the front pages of every newspaper in America."

Tom glanced at his watch. "I'm out with Andy at six," he said. "We better get to it."

While Kelley puttered with the makings of coffee in the kitchen Don began to lay out methodically his case against the esteemed bishop. McTighue grew up in St. Ita parish in Uptown, the only son of immigrant parents who were almost forty when they married. His dad was a streetcar conductor and then a bus driver for the CTA. His mother took up sewing for the grand dames on Sheridan Road to augment the family income—which was spent mostly on young Michael, their only child, born in immigrant Irish tradition nine months and ten minutes after their wedding. How happy they must have been when at the age of ten he announced he wanted to become a priest. They bought him everything he needed to achieve that lofty goal. But young Michael McTighue was always embarrassed by their rough brogue and their simple ways and their modest apartment over a dry cleaner's on Broadway. Like so many others before him, he saw the priesthood as a way of elevating his status in society.

"His seminary classmates joked that he had his wrists pierced so he could still wear cufflinks with a short sleeve shirt," Don said with a wry smile.

McTighue apparently pushed himself hard into the fast lane after ordination, never content with being a mere "Father." He always had his eyes on an episcopal ring. A short but ridiculously lucrative first assignment was at St. Barnabas parish in the South Side's Beverly neighborhood, where his once-embarrassing parents' brogue would conveniently resonate in his voice when he was sharing a quiet moment with an older parishioner. He taught religion for two years at the high school seminary and, after additional advanced studies at the American College of Louvain, Belgium, was granted a not-unexpected appointment to the faculty of St. Mary of the Lake Seminary. Each move was carefully orchestrated to shift his career forward. But it still wasn't fast enough for him. He needed a sponsor, an angel, an influential prince of the church.

Don's eyes blazed as he told us how McTighue insinuated himself onto a national committee headed by a now disgraced cardinal from New England, even while he remained on the St. Mary seminary faculty. He started by exhibiting a stomach for the man's dirty work, using his well-documented talent for remembering names, faces, and, most of all, secrets. Soon the two of them were travelling to Rome together. McTighue quickly graduated from lackey to confidant. When he used all the tools at his disposal to break up an early lawsuit that would have discredited the cardinal, McTighue's elevation to the most exclusive men's club in the world became a foregone conclusion. Few were surprised when he was named an auxiliary bishop for Chicago, or when he landed his own diocese in Tulsa, Oklahoma. At a very young age he found himself racing down the fast track of ecclesial promotion. Distracted as he was by his growing responsibilities, he wasn't available to step in at a moment when the cardinal needed him most. His heavy-handed patron slipped up and, without McTighue to cover for him, fell from grace. As soon as the fall seemed inevitable, McTighue tried to distance himself, but Tulsa, hard by the banks of the Arkansas River, the Gateway to Green County, would turn out to be the highest arc of his previously meteoric career.

On the surface, McTighue's path to advancement was not all that unusual. Though a far cry from St. Paul's classic admonitions to his disciple Timothy, it was a path that many men took to become bishops. But what Don had in his attaché case was not so common: pages of documents describing the very expensive gifts McTighue showered on anyone he thought could help him, everything from Rolex watches to first-class airline tickets. The conundrum was that Mom and Dad McTighue had left their son a paltry estate of under $5,000, and he had never shown any legal income beyond his modest priest's salary. How did he have the wherewithal to be so generous?"

Kelley brought out a pot of coffee and made the rounds filling cups as Don finished his power analysis. "At least six Irish widows of St. Barnabas remembered him most generously in their wills. On separate occasions, two of them died on the steps of church before the early weekday Mass, in the dark. Both times the bodies were discovered by...anyone?... anyone?"

"Good Father Michael," I offered.

"Both times discovered by him when he was alone. A third was found in the church ladies room after Mass. By McTighue."

"Performing his customary pastoral duties inspecting the ladies room. Nothing suspicious about that," Tom said laconically.

"Still another was found slumped in her car in the church parking lot. She died before the ambulance, called by McTighue, arrived. There were more. One poor woman had a blocked vent in her Longwood Drive home's boiler and died of carbon monoxide poisoning one night after he brought her communion. And the last one died from a fire that seems to have started on her dresser in front of a melted statue of Mary and a charred photo of young Fr. McTighue."

"No one ever raised an eyebrow?" Mel asked.

"These were really old women," Don explained. "A parish like St. Barnabas has a couple funerals a week. Who investigates why the grass grows? And the accidents are not uncommon. There was never any suspicion of wrongful death."

"Why no autopsies?" Kelley asked. "I thought that was required if there was no attending physician at the time of death."

"'Attending physician' is defined pretty broadly by Illinois statute," Tom explained. "It doesn't mean the doctor was present. Just that he or she had seen the deceased in the last thirty days."

"Which a conniver like McTighue would make sure they had done," Kelley said.

"He probably drove them to their medical appointments," I said, "being the loving priest he was. Helped them manage their meds."

"Even if they had never seen a doctor," Tom said, "the Cook County ME has lots better ways to waste taxpayer's money than doing tox screens on ninety-year-old ladies who dropped dead saying the rosary. They would have been toe-tagged, rubber-stamped, and shipped out in twenty-four hours."

"So he gathers a small fortune in dead widows' purses," Don continued, "and begins to invest in real estate, buying himself a condo on Marine Drive in Chicago, another in Palms Springs, Florida, a farm in Door County, Wisconsin…something new every couple of years. He also accumulated a large portfolio of stocks that were given to him by other widows, sometimes at Christmas, or for his ordination anniversaries, or his episcopal consecration… The real estate purchases were usually made by cutouts, shell corporations, sometimes shells inside shells, but the real estate broker he used was the same one for all the purchases. D'Amato Realty, owned by Tony D'Amato, grandson of a former outfit accountant, Benny 'The Bean' D'Amato."

"Is he our mob link?" I asked.

Tom shook his head. "Not anymore. Benny's body was found floating down the Chicago River by a boatload of plumbers who were dyeing the river green last St. Patty's day. It's hard to say who's running the show now. Organized crime ain't really all that organized anymore."

"Now it starts to get interesting," Don said. "Five, six years ago the bishop suddenly dumped three properties for a hefty profit. He and Tony formed a new corporation they named the Blackhawk North Holding Company. They sold and resold the property to their different shells to make it look like the property was appreciating in value. They remained in the shadows while lieutenants ran the day-to-day operations. So Blackhawk North starts making some small purchases in Bridgeview. Some distressed individual residences, a few businesses, a trailer park. It was an area where the archdiocese was confidentially considering an income-producing, mixed-use development. They were going to create a hundred acres of single family homes, some high-density, affordable housing, and an outdoor mall with a couple of big-box stores and lots of national retail. At the center of it would be a new Pastoral Center for the archdiocese. And it would all be financed by somewhat exclusive retirement condos for well-to-do seniors (and good donors to the archdiocese) in the upper floors."

"McTighue didn't have the juice to push this in the Chicago Diocese," I said. "Who was pushing this inside?"

Don flicked his eyebrows and gave a wicked grin.

"One Billy Gallo." He refilled his coffee cup while we digested what he said. "It was his baby from the start. Whether or not he colluded, who knows? But McTighue got a whiff early on and smelled a chance to make a killing reselling property to the archdiocese. He didn't buy everything. Just enough that there was no way around him if the development was going to go through.

"In the end, Blackhawk North held out for so much more than the property was actually worth that the finance committee of the archdiocese balked. Then one day the cardinal himself announced that he was closing Quigley North and turning that facility into the new Pastoral Center. Ironically, there was an unrelated burp in the real estate market just when McTighue and company lost the opportunity to dump their holdings on the archdiocese. They were left holding the bag, and were upside down on a lot of overleveraged real estate nobody wanted to buy."

"Whoever inherited D'Amato's bit," Tom said, "could not have been happy about losing out on a sure thing—a sure thing that Mikey McTighue brought them into."

"McTighue had to be furious," Don said. "The Quigley facility, no matter how much was spent on it, was a cow he couldn't milk."

"How much of this was Waterman aware of?" I asked.

"We can't be sure. But he had a whiff of something. And an ax to grind with McTighue. And all the resources he needed to buy what information was out there."

"The mob has other resources, but I'm betting this busted McTighue out. It would explain his wild rant at the Pastoral Center," I said.

"The most recent evidence I just got from Tulsa shows an extraordinary amount of shifting funds and fiduciary irregularity there. It looks like McTighue recently reached the end of his rope and started floating diocesan funds to keep his boat afloat. He's probably hoping the market will rebound and he can repay them before anyone notices they're missing. So things were already starting to spiral out of control, when he gets wind that Cosmo is making a case for murder."

"How could he have known that?" Kelley asked. "We still haven't sprung our little trap."

"Three guesses," I said. She furrowed her brow at me. "Try going in alphabetical order," I added.

"Oh, my God! Andy."

"Playing all three sides against the middle," Tom said. "A very dangerous game indeed."

"But is McTighue far enough beyond the pale to order the hit on Joey Greco?" I said. "Could he kill someone?"

"It's not like it would be the first time," Don offered.

"Might not have been the last," I said.

CHAPTER TWENTY

I decided to take a bus to the Pastoral Center the next morning. For the foreseeable future my car would remain a risky option. My juices started to flow when I hit the cold air, and my head started to clear as I walked toward the bus stop, my breath steaming as I went. The idea was awakening in me that I still had a lot to prove. And I didn't just need to prove it to the others. I had to prove it to myself.

Most of the sidewalks were neither shoveled nor salted. The overnight cold had frozen them into a rutted and slippery challenge. Without fresh snow it was all starting to look dirty and depressing. At Clark Street I hopped onto an over-heated 22 bus. As we passed Wrigley Field I marveled at the thought that opening day was only six weeks away.

More than the overheated bus was making me uncomfortable this morning. It might have been my night away from the comforts of Jack. Or maybe it was the realization that the pathetic suicide of a lonely old man was morphing into something with far-reaching repercussions. Or my faltering hope that Don might finally begin to trust me. I've grown used to disappointing people; I'm not so used to having them put their faith in me. My jitters were edging toward paranoia. Why were the other passengers looking like hired killers? Was that Chevy Malibu I noticed out the back window still following the bus? And why wasn't the bus driver in full uniform?

I needed to get hold of myself and go over the plan we had hammered out for Gallo before splitting up late the night before.

The bus was already approaching downtown.

The Knights stepped in originally because they were determined to prevent a rogue bishop from causing a financial scandal. They thought they had a workable plan. Other players stepped in. No one is exactly sure who or why. We had pretty good, but not conclusive, evidence that it was someone from organized crime. Now we mainly wanted to make sure we protected ourselves. Maybe we could use those unknown operatives to help us reach our goals. If the Knights could remain in the background as events played out, maybe no more innocent people would get hurt. Maybe that was God's plan. It was mine anyway.

My first objective in meeting with Gallo was to find out how much of this mess he knew about. Second was to figure out whose side he was on. This was especially tricky, since I had no sure idea where the lines between the sides were drawn. I did know that McTighue's greed had ruined Gallo's dream of a shining city on the hill. The new Pastoral Center and the church-driven economic development in Bridgeview were to be his crowning achievement before retirement, an accomplishment befitting his huge ego. There would have been ribbon cuttings, television interviews, newspaper headlines, a black-tie testimonial dinner at the Peninsula Hotel, an audience with the pope, and a perpetual seat at the right hand of Jesus. We all agreed there should be no love lost between him and McTighue or the other shapeless denizens of the Blackhawk North Holding Company. But for all his flaws, Billy still seemed loyal to the church he had served faithfully for decades. By what calculus could you possibly find mob hit men and a pillar of the church like Gallo in the same equation? And how much did he know about his son-in-law's culpability? Was Andy the only one playing a dangerous game? My third goal in talking to Gallo was not to tip my hand about anything I knew.

The bus whipped though a field of a dozen careering cabs,

and pulled up with a shudder of the diesel engine at the corner of Clark and Chestnut. I looked at my watch. Ten minutes before eight, my appointed time. I got off the bus and was again amazed at how crowded the sidewalks were with people on their way to work, leaning into the biting wind that swooped down from the tall buildings around us. As I approached the Pastoral Center I spied a dark Impala with a whip antenna pulling out of the courtyard. From where I stood I could see McTighue in the back seat. He didn't look happy. He was looking straight ahead, so I doubted he saw me. Even if he did, he would not have recognized me. I did not get a good look at the driver, but from the angle I had it could have been Andy Morrissey. I couldn't tell for sure.

At exactly 8:00 a.m. I climbed the steps to the entrance of the Pastoral Center. Gallo was at the door. I was still feeling the disquietude I had experienced when I caught the bus, and felt a pang of anxiety as I climbed the steps. For a moment I was reminded of the way I felt the first time I climbed them, a fourteen-year-old in white socks and black pegged trousers, feeling wildly unprepared for the challenges that lay ahead.

"Grande. On time. I'm surprised. Quick, come in."

"And a good morning to you as well, Billy. I didn't know you doubled as the doorman."

He ignored my comment and jerked his head in a 'come on' gesture. He quickly led me, not up to his office, but downstairs to where I remembered the pool and showers and locker room used to be. A long forgotten sense of dread rose up in me anew. We walked in silence for a good five minutes. We passed no one. Nothing looked much like it did when I was a student, so I had no idea where he was leading me.

I followed him deep into the bowels of the old gothic building, and the basement halls continued to bring back distant, uncomfortable adolescent memories.

Still not speaking a word, he reached into his suit coat pocket and pulled out an impressive set of keys. He stopped in a far, dark corner of a dead-end hallway and unlocked an unmarked door. He stepped into a windowless room and turned on a light, a single, bare bulb hanging from a high ceiling. It swung now on its cord, making our shadows bob and weave across the floor. The room was simply furnished, with a dinged metal utility table directly under the central light and a metal chair on either side. I recognized the furniture from my high school days here. This seemed to be a room that even time had forgotten. I stopped dead in my tracks in the doorway, like a fourteen-year-old boy about to receive his come-uppance.

"For Christ sake, come in and sit down." Gallo had gained the upper hand and he knew it.

There were no piled carpets or brass sconces here, just slab cement painted institutional gray and white cinder block walls with no more ornamentation than a toilet stall. A large mirror on the far wall cast my beleaguered reflection back at me, and invited my speculation of watchers on the other side. In the mirror I spied my gray-headed figure sweating, breathing shallow, until at last it seemed to signal with a blank expression that I had to stop swilling down this tepid porridge from the past that Gallo was serving up. I needed to relax, to stay calm myself, to steady myself for the task at hand and follow last night's battle plan, despite this unanticipated den of inquisition. I took a deep breath and felt a little more myself, even under Billy Gallo's baleful gaze, one last, blunt arrow in his quiver of attempts at intimidation. I looked around at the bare, chipped walls and corners strung with the dust of old cobwebs.

"Love what you've done with the place," I said.

Gallo tried to remain calm. The only indication that my lack of respect—or fear—surprised him was the way the tips of his ears were starting to turn red. Everybody lies with their lips, and the good ones lie with their eyes, but nobody lies with their ears.

It's like a tell in poker, unconscious and irrepressible.

"Grande, you need to tell me right now what the hell is going on and I don't want to play any of your games. I know that Ed Waterman's death is still being investigated. I also know that your name has been taken off the cop's persons of interest list. Everyone has read about Joey Greco's murder. I also know that the cops found some unusual tampering done to your car. And I figure that must be why you're riding around in a cab with no medallion."

Listing his discoveries seemed to give him confidence and he curled his lips in what was almost, but not quite, a smile.

"Does Holy Mother Church now consider riding in an unlicensed cab a mortal sin?" What I really wanted to know was whether he had the taxi under surveillance when Kelley and Don got into it at my place. They were compromised if he did, and that had the potential of blowing our cover big time. "Since when did the Archdiocese of Chicago start tailing people?"

"Don't flatter yourself. We don't. But I have friends on the police force, friends who mark a cab parked in front of your condo. Not such a common thing, a parked cab. What good uniform wouldn't check it out? And then it's gone. And before his shift is over it's back again? It wasn't hard to put two and two together."

I nodded, as if in appreciation of his deductive powers.

"Never were no flies on you, Billy." That grimace of his that passed for a smile drew a little tighter.

"By now," he continued patronizingly, "you must know that Waterman had a grudge against McTighue. I confess that I didn't know much about Waterman's personal life, just that his foundation has been very generous to the diocese. Maybe he thought he could buy his way back into the priesthood. Between you and me, Cosmo, he probably could have if it weren't for McTighue. It appears that the esteemed bishop felt passionately that men who left the priesthood are deserters. Unfortunately for Waterman,

McTighue spooked the cardinal."

"Well, like it says on McTighue's coat of arms, 'you are a priest forever.'"

I was tossing him a little bait, trying to throw him off balance.

He bit. Gallo tried to disguise his surprise, but his pink ears squealed the truth like the little piggy going wee, wee, wee, all the way home. I had rattled him.

"Yah," he said, trying to brush it off. "Something like that. I guess you are right. In any case McTighue is up to his ears in all this without a paddle."

"You're mixing your metaphors, Billy. Where did you go to school?"

Could his ears get any redder without bursting into flame?

He ignored the jab and gave a sidelong glance in each direction, as if to assure himself the room was still empty. "Cosmo, what I am about to tell you is strictly between you and me."

"And the man behind the mirror."

My eyes caught his in its reflection. They were clear and ice blue and there was nothing pretty to see there.

"McTighue's has been stealing from the church," he said. "Here and out west. We can confront him privately, to get him to retire. And then quietly send reserve cash out to Tulsa to avert a scandal. But it's imperative we know who killed Waterman. I can't put it past McTighue. But if we are to contain this we need to know who else knows what's going on. Justice is going to be done, but you have to tell me, just what do you know?"

"Give me one reason in the world why should I tell you *all* that I know?" I purposely emphasized the word *all*. "And why should I give a rat's ass if some rogue bishop gets himself caught with his hand in the collection basket? Frankly, I'm dead weary of car bombs, and old friends getting executed, and mostly of Waterman hanging around like Marley's ghost on Christmas Eve."

I stood up so quickly that it startled him. "This much I will tell you." I stopped and walked over to the mirror, watching my reflection as I flipped my middle finger at whoever was on the other side. "I know that you and I are being watched. And I know just who is on the other side watching and listening to us," I lied. "And I'm damn tired of this amateur attempt to squeeze information out of me."

That was true enough. I was beginning to feel like I was on a roll, no longer cowed, but drawing energy from the adrenalin jolt I'd gotten from being dragged into a dark basement from my past. I was as proud of what I left unsaid as what I had just shouted at him. The red from his ears spread across his face and began morphing towards a deep purple. He stood and leaned on the table as if he needed its support to hurl at me the words he really wanted to say.

"Listen, you little *pothead*. I'm *glad* they never ordained you. I've worked *too long* and *too hard* for the church or me to be brought down by the likes of you and Waterman and McTighue. The church is *too important* to me…"

He seemed to almost choke on the words. What started loud and intensified now became a hissing whisper, "and so is family, my family. Do you hear me? If there is going to be more bloodshed, it won't be on my hands. I can only do so much. I cannot be responsible for the actions of others." He must have realized how vulnerable he sounded, so he upped the volume again. "I have insulated myself from this abrogation of all that is right and holy. I wash my hands of it." He wiped his palms together as if to rid himself of the dirt of this wicked world for once and for all. He tugged at his shirt, which had ridden up in his moment of ire, and straightened his jacket on his shoulders. "My advice to you, Grande, is to stop running around like the Lone Ranger, casting unfounded aspersions at your betters. You'll take that advice if you know what's good for you."

He turned with what dignity he could muster and walked out the door. I offered one last scowl at the mirror, needing to conceal the smile trying to force its way across my face. I hadn't told Gallo anything that he didn't already know. And he had no idea how much he had told me.

CHAPTER TWENTY-ONE

10:15 found me on West North Avenue, hard by the lake shore, riding a glass elevator up the side of a luxury apartment building to the apartment of Felix "The Nose" La Nasa, mafioso emeritus, an old timer who had once controlled a fair share of the Chicago mob. Lincoln Park fell below me as I rose. From twenty-six stories up, its snow-covered meadows looked as white and pure as Bethlehem on Christmas morning.

I had not seen La Nasa since before his vaunted retirement some ten or fifteen years earlier. He married outside the fold, an Irish girl, and his daughter Mary Catherine had hired me to get the goods on her philandering and abusive husband back in the eighties. She knew better than to turn to Daddy, who would have taken the miscreant perch fishing on Lake Michigan and dumped him twenty miles east of Kenosha with the laces of his Louis Vuitton Blasters tied together in a double knot. Things turned out well for Mary Catherine. I...persuaded...her hubby not just once, but twice, to at least stop shoving her around, and the second conversation, which ended up costing him a couple thousand in bridgework, took. She kept my business card stuck to the refrigerator after that, and ten weeks later hubby moved to Albuquerque for the air.

Felix eventually got wind of what I had done. He was never a man to let a personal kindness go unrewarded. A guy in a beaten pork pie hat and an ill-fitting polyester suit with bad breath and good manners walked into my office one day and said, "Excuse me, sir. I'm looking for Mr. Grande."

"You're all done. That's me."

He thumped a paper lunch bag on my desk. It wasn't real light.

"Compliments of Mr. La Nasa," he said.

I peaked in the bag. Uncirculated fifties. Still in Department of the Treasury wrappers.

"What have I gotta to do for it?"

"It's for past favors, sir. No strings attached. With his compliments. Family is very important to Mr. La Nasa. You got his daughter out of a mess, apparently. He thanks you."

He tipped his hat and walked out without another word.

I bought my Jack out of that bag for ten years. I even called in a marker once or twice when I accidentally got mixed up with some guys a lot badder than me. I hadn't spoken to Felix for so long that I wasn't even sure he was still alive when I called the day before to ask for the appointment.

I had my doubts that I would actually learn anything useful today. The Nose had to be twenty years out of touch with the day-to-day. But I was pretty sure I could get him to deliver a message I wanted very badly to deliver.

A slender, pretty woman with cinnamon skin and an island accent answered my ring. Her hair was pulled into a tight bun and she wore cream-colored haram pants, a white satin blouse, and a cornflower blue blazer.

"Mr. Grande," she said, "please come in. Mr. La Nasa is waiting for you in the back room."

I expected to find La Nasa in a wheel chair with an Afghan thrown across his lap, but he was sitting in a scroll foot chair in a pool of sunlight looking like he was at the club waiting for a tennis court to open up. He was lean and white haired and wore a crimson eye patch he had never worn before. He stood and smiled at my approach.

"Good to see you, Cosmo."

"Likewise, sir. You're looking well."

"Melanoma," he said, waving a finger at the eye, addressing the elephant in the room.

He waved me into a seat near the window. Below us, the Gold Coast lay resplendent in morning sunlight, and the low sun cast a great band of light along the broad bight of lake shore just to the south.

"How are you, Cosmo?"

"*Testa dura,*" I said. Hardheaded. Or, less literally, but more to the point, pigheaded.

"With people from Bari, how else could you be?"

"How are Mary Catherine and the kids?"

"You know she remarried."

"And well. A neurosurgeon."

"Head of neurosurgery now at Missouri Baptist. Kids are grown. Do you believe I have two great-grandkids? I'm not doin' too bad for an old geezer of ninety-two."

"You don't look a day over ninety-one," I said, and laughed.

"To what do I owe the honor?"

"I'm working on a very confusing case. One that might have brushed against some people connected to your old outfit."

"What outfit would that be? I was in environmental waste management."

I smiled. "All right. A case in which I might have brushed against some environmental waste managers then." His turn to smile. "I wouldn't expect you to tell me about any friends. But from what I read in the paper about your retirement, I thought you might have left some people behind that you weren't too friendly with."

"That was all such a long time ago. Why bear a grudge?"

"Still, if I throw some facts out there, and if you felt like sharing anything, it would be a favor between friends."

He shrugged. The woman who had answered the door

brought two espressos unbidden, and I noticed a bulge in the back of her blazer as she bent to serve Felix. A small bulge. A .32 automatic, my bet. Maybe some ancient grudges were still unsettled. It gave me new hope for my cause.

"Do you know a realtor named a Tony D'Amato?" I decided to start with the one name I knew he would know.

"I knew his old man pretty good. And his grandfather. Tony came later. He might have been at Mary Catherine's wedding. The real one. I don't really remember, and don't think I ever spoke to him."

"The people I am investigating might have worked with him and are involved in a real estate inflation scheme down in Bridge-view."

This drew a stare so blank I thought at first he might be having a petit mal seizure. I moved on.

"You ever heard of a Blackhawk North Holding Company?"

"Do they own the hockey team?"

I read a list of names of businesses I had found associated with Blackhawk North Holding Company. Much as I expected, he shook his head at each like he was shaking a fly off his ear.

"Ancovia Bank?" Shake. "Guardian Trust?" Shake. "Cayman Eleuthera Bank?"

"That's the whole problem with the world today," he said. "It makes me glad I got out of it at such a young age." He had been seventy-eight or so, as I remembered. "Things used to be simple. You ran your book. You had your crews showing up with bags of money. You never even had to push that many people around. I blame the unions. Once the kids figured out that they could sit in their office with a Starbucks and a bran muffin, resting their thumb on a $300 million pension fund, why they wanna go out at four o'clock in the morning and hijack a truckload of televisions?" He threw both hands forward in a gesture of dismissal. "Life just got so complicated. Simple is better, Cosmo. Simple is better. All these young Turks with their computers and their investment schemes. Since Joe Batters died you don't even know who's in charge anymore. In my day people knew who the hell was in charge." He twisted a lemon rind over his cup and took a sip.

"You still talk to people, though. People you could warn if they were getting in over their heads."

"I have a lot of friends."

"Well you might let friends know that whatever is going on down there is about to blow wide open. A lot of serious people, and I don't mean local law enforcement, have an interest in getting to the bottom of this case. I'm talking about players. Men of influence. CEO's from all over the country. And there has already been one killing. One that was completely unnecessary. Not a soldier. Not some dirty cop or probation officer they got in their pocket. A civilian. A goddamn mechanic. And a personal friend of mine."

"That's too bad. I'm sorry to hear that."

"There's going to be one hell of a mess to clean up. It would be better for everyone if it didn't get any messier."

The lady in the blue blazer walked in.

"Mr. La Nasa, it's time for your aspiration."

He nodded but waved her away.

"I'll see what I can do," he said. "I've never forgotten what you did for us. I know if I had known about it at the time, and handled it myself, I wouldn't have the relationship I have with my daughter today. You're one of the good guys, Cosmo. I know that if I know nothing else."

CHAPTER TWENTY-TWO

I was on the train back to my place, feeling like a man on the side of the angels for once, when my cell phone buzzed in my pocket. Don's name and number lit up the display but the ringtone "Pomp and Circumstance" had already told me it was him. In a moment of whimsy, or drunkenness (probably both, as I do not remember doing it), I had set some new ring tones on my cell.

"I've been waiting to hear from you. Where the hell are you?"

"The El," I confessed, with the clatter of wheels in the background. I was glad he didn't ask which train.

"Are you being followed?"

"Who you talking to, Don?"

"All right. Sorry. I'm just getting used to sober Cosmo. So you survived your confrontation with Gallo unscathed. Tell me about it."

I described the basement interrogation room where Gallo had taken me.

"I know the place," he said. "There have been all sorts of crazy rumors about it. The legend is that it's where they break down pedophile priests and other enemies of the faith. I thought the stories were always a bit too bizarre to be true. Still, whenever I'm down that way, someone always seems to stop and redirect me. Is there really a one way mirror?"

"Does the pope wear funny hats?"

"So what did he say?"

"It's a little complicated for the phone. We need to talk face to face. But first send our friend Mel on a long drive in the country. Gallo's onto him. Well, not completely onto him, maybe, but he knows the cab is a fake. When can we meet?"

"There's a 5:00 p.m. Mass at St. Ignatius Church in Rogers Park, in their side chapel. Pretend like you're going in the side door of the church for Mass, but instead of going up the stairs, go down to the Holy Name Society's clubhouse. We'll all be there."

"I almost forgot. I saw your friend Bishop McTighue in the back seat of an unmarked squad car coming out of the Pastoral Center before I met with Gallo. He didn't look very happy. And, I'm pretty sure Andy was doing the driving."

"You're right. He took McTighue to the Town Hall police station on Addison. Not sure why there and not the department's South Loop Headquarters. My guess is that they don't want to be seen together."

"How did you know all that?"

"Haven't you figured out we got eyes everywhere, man? The night watchman in the Pastoral Center is one of us, and the desk sergeant at Town Hall is an old friend from my days on the bench. You say McTighue didn't see you. Did anyone see you and Gallo together?"

"Nope. He made sure of that."

"Good. Lay low until tonight. Don't go home or to your office. You might pick up a tail. Window shop or go to the Art Institute or hit an early movie. Better yet, get a damn haircut."

As Don suggested I rode the train right past the stops for my condo and office, with no more thought than to ride around until I came to some place where I could get a stiff drink. Or a good haircut.

Just past Diversey my cell phone sounded. The theme from "Hawaii Five-0" told me Tom was on the line.

"What's up?"

"Where are you right now?"

"Red Line, north of the river."

"What the hell are you doing there?"

"Visiting a sick friend."

"Headed which way?"

"South."

"Good. Head down to Water Tower Place. Go in the main entrance and take the escalator up to the main floor, then take the back escalator down to the food court. Relax. Have a cup of coffee. Look like you're loafing. At 1:00 p.m. exactly, take the parking garage elevator down to the fourth level. I'll be waiting for you there in an unmarked car. If you sense that anyone has been following you, keep going. Got it?"

"Okay. But where are we going?"

"A rolling safe house. We stash witnesses there. Sometimes a rogue cop will take an uncooperative witness there to iron the starch out of him. For the past few weeks we've been using a house on Kenmore just north of Argyle. The Vietnamese around there are pretty good at minding their own business. And as luck would have it, it's on the way to St. Ignatius."

"Why are we going there?"

"It's just a hunch. But with any luck at all, we may find Andy there. And McTighue. Or what's left of them."

"You're not suggesting…"

"There's some very bad people out there, Cosmo. Some very bad people."

———

Your average suburban shopping mall is a pretty fine place to spot a tail. Lots of interesting, reflective windows to stop at innocently while you wait to see if anybody behind you makes a sudden stop or turn. And the long strips invite you to slap your head, turn around like you forgot something, and walk the other way. Right past anyone who might be tailing you, or someone walking against the grain on the other side of the mall. If they are any good you probably won't be able to pick them out, but they will have to lay way back after passing face to face. But Water Tower Place, Chicago's basilica of high-end consumerism for well-heeled tourists and their spoiled children, is all vertical. Its eight-floor rotunda makes it a lot tougher to spot a tail. Someone could have eyes on you from three floors up.

I looked up the number for the closest Morton's and spent a couple futile minutes talking to them on speaker, as if trying to convince the maître d' to deliver a medium-rare 24-ounce porterhouse and a chocolate soufflé to the food court. What I was actually doing was recording a video of people passing me in both directions, with special attention to their shoes. A skilled operative can change his or her appearance several times in a minute—don a hat, lose a jacket, change glasses—but I never met one yet who changed shoes. I headed down to the food court and ordered an eight-ounce bottle of San Pellegrino with a twist of lime that set me back as much as a three-finger Jack during happy hour at St. Martin's Inn.

I found myself a seat at a little bistro table off in a corner where I could pass the time running my little video and checking out anyone who passed by. I never saw the same pair of Keds twice. No one was tailing me. I looked at my watch every few minutes. At 1:00 sharp I swallowed the last of the bottled water and headed over to the parking garage elevators. I called the elevator and waited alone until I stepped into the car. No one followed me. I waited until the door closed to choose my floor and when the doors opened Tom was in the driving lane outside the elevator in an idling Impala. Like most cops he was a great driver. Within two minutes of leaving the garage he had swung effortlessly on to northbound Lake Shore Drive.

"Think anyone followed you?" His first words. It had taken

him to North Avenue to say anything. He clearly had something on his mind.

"Not to worry. I left a note on the table in the food court saying where we were going." I got a trace of a smile from him.

"You're a funny guy, Cosmo, a real barrel of yucks. Look how I'm laughing. I've been checking the rearview mirror. I'm pretty sure we're in the clear. If anyone was trying to follow you they'd be watching the doors to public transportation."

He made me wish I wore glasses so I could pull them down to the end of my nose and give him a stern look over the top of the frame. "Nobody. Followed. Me."

He shrugged acceptance at last, but still kept one eye on the mirror.

He got off Lake Shore Drive at Belmont and turned north on Halsted, taking us through what was affectionately called "Boys' Town," the gay neighborhood adjoining the ball park.

"Love the short cut," I said.

"There's nothing wrong with being extra careful."

Then it was back to silence. I learned years ago that when Tom didn't want to talk, you might as well be sitting next to a garden gnome. He deked onto North Broadway and headed dead west on Argyle before turning north onto Kenmore. Gentrification was just starting to reshape the architectural and human landscape. A few faded mansions sat alongside new condos, and Chicago-style four-plus-ones were boarded up next to refurbished hotels that had chopped their suites up into cheap studio apartments. Many blocks had a dumpster at the curb where fearless entrepreneurs chased the Yankee dollar. The best thing that had happened to the neighborhood was the influx of Vietnamese after the war. Their buildings were pristine and even in the dead of winter you could tell the landscaping had been trimmed to within an inch of its life.

Tom turned the unmarked squad car into an alley where we

bumped along over the grooves dug into the ice. Neither of us had said a word in the last ten minutes. While I had let my mind wander, Tom seemed intense and a bit nervous. He parked the car behind the garage of a two-flat, effectively hiding it from view. An elderly Asian woman who might have been fifty or might have been ninety waved a friendly hello from behind a closed window. Tom waved back, nodding.

"We're going four houses up the street. Follow me. We'll take the gangways and backyards so nobody will see us."

"She just did."

"Not to worry, Cosmo. Fifty bucks from the Police Safety Fund hides our car from the street and guarantees that she will keep her mouth shut. We know what we are doing."

Tom led the way along a well-trodden path through deep snow. We stopped when we reached the backyard of an apparently abandoned two-story brick Georgian. A century ago it had been a stately single-family home. If it didn't get torched by its current owners or wasn't set afire by street people trying to stay warm, it had a good chance of becoming a neat and compact four-unit building with names like Thieu and Nguyen on the mailbox.

But now it was a place where cops stashed witnesses in jeopardy, or where a few took miscreants for extra-judicial remedies. I'm not naïve. For every hundred good cops like Tom there are a few who go sour, who joined the force for more than the noble reason to "serve and protect." Some just have fun pushing people around. I get it. I've had a little fun doing that myself.

The building at first appeared to be sealed tight. Tom stopped before a stairless basement door well.

"Open sesame?" I said.

"You sprain your ankle I'm leaving you here," he said, and jumped into the empty well.

I followed him into the hole, taking care to bend my knees

on impact from the half-story drop of six or seven feet.

"You planning to fly out of this pit?"

"Come on. Let's go find the pendulum."

Tom reached into his pocket for a key, but I noticed the door gapped a little at the jamb. I pressed on the door and it swung open.

"That's not good," Tom said.

He pressed me aside and drew his gun. He started through the door then paused, frowned, and shook his gun in the space between us. Duh! I drew my .38 and we stepped into a dark basement. Just a few bands of light leaked through the gaps in the boarded windows and a single large hole in the ceiling. Tom obviously knew where we were going. He led the way up a flight of concrete steps into what had once been a kitchen, now stripped to the studs. The copper plumbing had been plundered and bare knob-and-tube wiring was strung through the joists. A set of narrow stairs in the far corner continued up to the second floor at a steep angle. These must have been the back stairs used by the maids. The stairway was windowless, and we climbed in darkness, running a hand against one wall for guidance.

At the head of the stairs Tom paused, listening. He leaned forward on the steps and put an ear to the gap at the bottom of the door. There was enough light that I could see him close his eyes and pinch his nose, swallow, and open his mouth wide. It's an old cop's trick for hearing what you might not otherwise hear. It opens the tube that connects your ear and mouth, makes your ear drum a little more sensitive, and your open mouth may help sound resonate like the body of a guitar. All I could hear was the pounding of my own heart. I kept trying to convince myself I was having fun, but wasn't doing a very good job.

Tom tugged at the door and it opened towards us. We stepped into a wide hallway. All but one of the doors on both sides of the hallway were closed. Tom pointed to the open door with the barrel of his service revolver and nodded to me. That's where we were going. We inched our way toward it. I was surprised that there was no squeaking coming from the old wooden boards underfoot. We spun into the open doorway.

Tom's voice broke the silence. "Damn it!"

We stood in what must have once been the master bedroom. Just as in the rest of the house, the windows were boarded. A plank high on one bay window was missing, and light fell as if from a dim spotlight onto an old wooden stool lying on its side in the middle of the room in a blackening puddle of blood. Motes of dust spun in the band of light from the window and in the eerie silence I thought I heard the ticking of a watch.

Tom stooped and tapped a finger at the puddle of blood.

"Half an hour," he said. "Maybe a little more."

I was still holding my gun out in front of me in both hands. "Where do you think they took the body?"

"They?"

I pulled a foot across the dusty floorboards. "Lots of footprints. No drag marks."

Tom nodded. "If there was a body to dispose of it took at least two men. But I'm not sure anyone was killed here. There's not enough blood. Whoever sat on the stool was probably slapped around a bit. But there was no stabbing or battering with a baseball bat. The blood didn't splatter. It just dripped."

I took a breath and brought the gun down to my side. "You think it was the kid?"

"We pulled the plug on this place a week ago. Some of the neighbors were starting to get nosy. But remember, I told you Andy took personal time this week, so he might not have known that we shut it down. Something else points to him. He's the kind of cop who likes to rough people up. He says it works and that the fear of getting it again keeps them quiet after. But there's only ever been one good reason to torture someone."

"What's that?"

"Because you enjoy doing it."

"What could Andy want to get from McTighue that he doesn't already have?" I said.

"Don't forget that McTighue isn't even a blip on the department's radar. There's a good chance that Andy might be doing some kind of extracurricular work here. Remember, he's everybody's boy. And we think he's killed once already."

"Let's see if they left anything behind. The kid is smart enough to wear gloves. And he would have cuffed McTighue before bringing him here. So there's probably no sense in you having the place dusted for prints."

Tom began a careful survey of the room, starting at the doorway we came through.

"You could type that blood," I said.

"A step ahead of you," he said, concentrating on his survey of the room.

I walked over to the stool. "May I?" Tom nodded. I carried it over to the spot where the sunlight was coming in. It wasn't all that bright so I felt around with my ungloved right hand and found the point of a nail that was sticking up through the top of the stool. I felt around it more gingerly and found something soft sticking to the nail. "You got light?" I said. Tom tossed me a small aluminum penlight. I popped it on and shone it on the point of the nail. "Look at this." A tuft of black fabric hung from the point of the nail.

"Don't get too excited, Cosmo. There's no way to tell if that cloth got caught on the nail today. It could have been there for years."

"Oh yah? I beg to differ." I picked the tuft from the stool. "What I am holding in my hand appears to be a piece of the finest black wool gabardine money can buy. McTighue prided himself in being an impeccable dresser. I'm guessing that a new pair of custom-made pants will set him back a bundle."

"If he's still alive."

"The tear has to be off the pants seat," I said. "At least it won't show in a casket."

"Always looking at the bright side, aren't you, Cosmo?"

CHAPTER TWENTY-THREE

We retraced our steps to the first floor and let ourselves out through a door off the pantry that opened with a panic bar from the inside but was stripped of knob or latch on the outside. A couple of days of good behavior were beginning to wear on me. I needed a drink.

"I feel like walking," I said to Tom. "Clears the head. I'll catch up with you at St. Ignatius."

He arched an eyebrow at me. "Sober, right?"

"How else."

"Skunk-face drunk, Cosmo. That's how else. Who you talking to?"

"Sober then. Scouts honor."

I walked toward Clark Street and the Andersonville neighborhood that lay between me and East Rogers Park. For a basically lazy guy, I don't mind walking. I never did. But it was getting noticeably colder. The sidewalk ruts had hardened. And still I had no gloves.

Once a hearty Swedish community where the shop owners responded to a bell ringer walking down Clark Street at ten on the dot every morning to wash down the sidewalks in front of their establishments, Andersonville had recently evolved into a dove cote of hip restaurants, bars, boutiques, and trendy shops fueled by the considerable spendable income of lesbians and, later, gay men forced out of Lakeview by rising rents. It had evolved into a lower key version of Boys' Town.

Thinking about my much-needed libation, I found an embarrassment of opportunities before me. I settled on the woody bar at Calo's restaurant and settled comfortably on a stool that allowed me to watch the parade of bundled up folks gritting their teeth as they streamed past the window, heads down into the sharp north wind. It was getting brutal out there. I knew that no matter how warm I was able to get myself sitting here the long walk up Clark Street to St. Ignatius was going to chill me to the bone.

A bartender wearing an Illinois Wesleyan sweatshirt and a phony grin came over and took my order, a double Jack Daniels, straight up, water back, no ice. The drink arrived in the nick of time with an insincere, "I'm Jerry. Just holler if you need anything." Before I could even administer a first dose, my cell phone rang. The "Forever Young" ring tone told me it was Kelley.

"Just leave the check when you got the time," I said to Jerry. I looked at my watch. "I'm in a little bit of a hurry."

"Let me guess," I said to Kelley. "You're out of the office and on your way to the El, right?"

"In this weather? You really are a lousy detective."

"That opinion is polling pretty well this week. How was Gallo after our meeting this morning?" I hoped her read of him might be able to give us a clue about what to do next. Sometimes detective work is like fishing without bait. You don't get a bite, but there's always a chance something will snag the line.

"I didn't see more than two minutes of him all day. He kept one or two phone lines busy all day. He made me cancel all his appointments. He only saw the cardinal, who didn't phone ahead like he usually does, and walked right past me without so much as a 'kiss my ring.'"

"I wonder what that's about?"

"Listen, Cosmo. I don't want to sound paranoid, but I could have sworn someone followed me when I went out to lunch today. I think I may have seen him before somewhere. It was so cold I just went next door and picked up a sandwich to bring back to the office. He was still standing outside in the cold when I walked out of the deli. I saw him again from the doorway at the Pastoral Center. He was half a block down Rush Street. I caught his eyes and he lowered his head, turned, and walked in the opposite direction."

"Would you recognize him if you saw him again?"

"Absolutely.

"Aren't you afraid he'll follow you to St. Ignatius?"

"Not to worry. I'm not walking in this weather. I borrowed a car from someone who decided to stay in the city tonight. He drove it into the courtyard for me. My shadow will be expecting me to leave on foot. Pretty good, huh?"

"Just be careful." I toyed with the notion to have her pick me up, but didn't want to admit I'd stopped for refreshments. "I'll see you at St. Ignatius soon." I chugged the last of my drink, buttoned my coat, left Jerry a decent tip, and got slammed in the face by the bitter cold as I stepped out of Calo's. I had a tough walk ahead of me.

It seemed to take forever just to reach the northern end of Andersonville. At one point I turned my head from a wind that was making my eyes tear. Over my shoulder I saw a figure walking in my direction. He looked abruptly away. He was about a half block back. With no one else walking on the street I glanced back a few times and he was always that same distance behind me. I was being followed. When I got to the Raven Theater at the corner of Clark and Granville, I turned east.

I picked up my pace as I walked past Hayt Elementary. The guy quickened his pace. A block later I was on the corner of Granville and Glenwood. There stood massive St. Gertrude church, looking every inch the great urban Catholic church it is. If I'd been ordained, that's where I would have wanted to be assigned. I walked past the rectory and its barren garden. Lovely

166

in summer, it was desolate and unwelcoming as an arctic tundra today.

I said a quick prayer that the doors to the church would be unlocked. I was not unfamiliar with St. Gert's, and confident I could shake my tail inside. The doors of the church were locked. I added my latest supplication to a long list of unanswered prayers and looked up to see my pursuer round the corner. We were less than fifty yards apart. He had given up any hope that I hadn't spotted him, but seemed to have no intention of assault. He just wanted to keep me from going where I wanted to go at this point. I took my bearings and remembered there was often a cab hanging around the Granville Medical Center a few blocks east. I turned onto North Broadway and saw not one, but two hacks. I walked up to the driver's window of the first cab and proffered a twenty dollar bill.

"Take a break," I said.

"I just had my dinner," he said, confused. He looked behind me like I had something funny going on.

"Get lost," I said, throwing the twenty in his lap. "Five minutes." He fishtailed out of his spot and spun down North Broadway.

I jumped into the last cab on the block. "St. Ignatius Church, up Glenwood, past Devon." I rolled down the window and flipped my follower the bird. "Drive safe," I told the driver. "I'm a big tipper."

I gave the driver a twenty when I got out at St. Ignatius and followed Don's instructions to a tee. I walked into the back side door of the church, massive as St. Gertrude, maybe even bigger. I slipped in the side door and down a flight of steps to a closed door. It swung open easily. The room was empty of human occupants, but I saw a light coming from under a door at the opposite end of the room. I opened the door without knocking and walked in.

Tom was sitting alone on the edge of a dented metal table talking on the phone. He nodded hello and a minute later ended his call.

The door behind me opened and Kelley entered the room, her eyes sparkling and her cheeks red from the cold.

"Don is stopping for food," Tom said. "He should be here any minute. Mel went for a drive."

He had no sooner spoken than we heard footsteps in the room outside. Don walked in empty handed.

"Damn, man," Tom said. "Where's my fried chicken?"

"There's not going to be any fried chicken. McTighue is dead."

CHAPTER TWENTY-FOUR

Ow?" I asked.

"Crashed his Caddie into a bus a couple hours ago. Dead on the scene. That's all I know right now." Don turned to Tom. "I'm sure you can get more."

The five of us stood there in the kitchen in an awkward moment of silence, not knowing exactly what to say or do. Or to feel. McTighue's death hung like the period at the end of a very long sentence. Or was it a question mark?

"The man we were chasing to ruin is a ghost," I said.

"God have mercy on his soul," Kelley said.

Tom rose to his feet. "There's nothing more to do here. We should all just go home. I'll find out what I can."

Don told Mel to follow Kelley while she returned her borrowed car. He gave him instructions to drive her home, secure her apartment, and stay outside her high rise for the night. Don, offered police protection by Tom, politely refused.

"I need some time without anyone in my face, including the police," he said pointedly.

"You're with me," Tom said to me, and I followed him out to his car.

Lake effect snow had started up again, tiny icy pellets furring the sidewalks and the car-clogged streets as we headed to my place. Tom invited himself in for a nightcap when we got back to Wrigleyville. I really wanted to be alone, but knew better than to tell him that. We sat in my living room for a while quietly, in the kind of silence that is not uncomfortable between good friends, each of us lost in our own thoughts. I rolled and fired up a joint. Without a word we passed it back and forth. Forty years drifted away. We were both doing our own thinking and knew we probably couldn't be much help to each other. Waterman's suicide, Joey's execution, and now McTighue's untimely demise. All under my nose and on Tom's watch. What next?

I turned on the TV to see if they had the story yet. A talking head with a $400 haircut reported that the police officially were calling it a "tragic accident." A crawl at the bottom of the screen quoted a prepared statement from the cardinal mourning the loss of a "native son, a true Chicagoan, a loyal servant of the church who will be greatly missed in Tulsa." That was it. Each word had been carefully scripted. There was no mention of his whereabouts in the hours before the accident, the wild ride with Andy, or the quick stop at a torture chamber in Little Saigon. The talking head was left with a minute of air time, and vamped with stories about the times he had met the prince of the church. The anchorman, mercifully, cut him off with a muttered "How sad." Was he talking about the death or the reporting of it?

I turned the TV off. Tom called police headquarters for more details. He turned the phone's speaker on while a bored voice summarized the official report.

"Bishop Michael McTighue left his rental car in the courtyard of the Pastoral Center overnight...spent the night at Holy Name Cathedral a few blocks from there."

Nothing too odd about that. That's the usual place for visiting bishops to stay. But this guy was a son of Chicago. I found it strange that he had no friends or family to stay with. Hell, even Steve Bartman can find a couch to crash on for a couple nights. The cop droned on.

"A statement from a nun who cooks at the place says he told her he would be out all day, but didn't say where. He wasn't seen leaving, or returning later for his vehicle, a rented Cadillac XTS, black. He drove north on Lake Shore Drive, was exiting at Hollywood when he rear-ended an out-of-service articulated CTA bus. It appeared that he was doing over fifty miles an hour at the moment of impact. No skid marks."

Tom raised his eyebrows at that.

"He was not wearing a seat belt, was thrown through the windshield, impacting the rear of the CTA vehicle with lethal force. The car's fuel tank ruptured and by the time emergency services arrived it was engulfed in flames. I seen this myself, after," the man reporting to us said. "That friggin' car was a puddle by the time they got the fire out."

"What about the bus driver?"

"Left the scene. And, the CTA has no record it was even checked out of the barn! Nobody knows what the bus was doing there."

"Suicide by bus?" Tom said.

"Not my job, man. Check with the medical examiner in a day or two. That's as much as I got, Tom. If that's all, we're kinda busy around here."

"Sure, Leo. Thanks a ton. Love to Celia." He hung up the phone.

"We got enough red flags here for a May Day parade in Moscow," I said.

We both sat silently trying to absorb what we just heard.

Tom broke the ice. "Don was right. There really were a lot of people who wanted McTighue silenced. So was this really an accident? And what did he share, sitting on the stool on Kenmore, that left him expendable? And who was there with him?"

"The church stopped murdering bishops a long time ago. And as for the mob, they've been trending legit ever since Tony Accardo died in his sleep. Would they risk all the public scrutiny around a murdered bishop? For what benefit?"

"So, Cosmo, if it wasn't an accident and wasn't set up by Holy

Mother Church or by the mob, who did it and why?"

"Gallo? Do you think he has the connections to pull something like this off?"

"If Andy's involved Gallo's got the only connection that matters. But for Gallo to use his own son-in-law...I stumble at that."

I was tempted to roll another joint but decided instead that we both needed a bracer. I went to the kitchen and brought out my old friend Jack. I rattled ice into two tumblers and poured two stiff drinks and returned the bottle to the kitchen cabinet. I came back and handed one of the glasses to Tom. He took it without a word. I took a good swallow from mine and savored the smoky essence of it.

"Maybe Gallo wasn't pushing Andy on this," I said. "Maybe it's just one rogue cop working solo. Figures he's doing his father-in-law a favor by making a mess go away."

"He could have tampered with McTighue's car easily enough. He knows his way around an automobile. I've got people checking what's left of the car."

"You know what they're going to find."

"So what happens if we link the kid to both the shooting of Joey Gallo and McTighue's 'accident'?" He rose and stretched. "I was just getting used to having the little bastard around. Now I'm gonna have to be the guy who drops him down a hole."

CHAPTER TWENTY-FIVE

When Tom was gone I topped my drink from his untouched glass and settled in my favorite chair. I wanted to sleep, but couldn't shake the expression on McTighue's face as I saw him as he was being driven out of the Pastoral Center. I got enough of the Jack in me at last and must have dozed off. I had a visit from McTighue's ghost, bloody and burnt, babbling in some ancient tongue I didn't understand. I saw Joey Greco slumped over the wheel of his tow truck with two tiny holes in one side of his head and a black, seeping exit wound gaping on the other.

Around three in the morning I awoke and walked to the living room window and looked out. The old double-hung windows leaked frigid air into the room. Damn if it wasn't snowing again. There was no wind to speak of. Big wet flakes were dropping fast but straight and the amber glow of sodium-vapor streetlights gave the fresh coating of snow an almost otherworldly look. Every car on the street was covered with a pristine layer of fresh snow. There were no footprints on the sidewalks and barely a tire track in the street. The heavy snow suppressed all the usual churning sounds of life in the big city, and the silence loomed as heavy as the falling snow. I felt entirely alone in the world, shuddering at my window and thinking in that moment of preternatural silence about nothing more than death in the cold Chicago winter.

The blizzard that began in the middle of the night was in full force when I opened the front door and stepped outside early the next morning. I'd been wakened by the chime of a text from Kelley, summoning me to meet her at Julius Meinl's Coffee Shop. The morning snow lay heavily on every rail and tree branch as I tramped to my car, still very much alone in the world, the only creature stirring in Chicago. There wasn't so much as a shoveler in sight, no blare of snowblower, or light scraping of steel shovel blades. The stillness gave me another shudder. I cleared the snow from the windshield with the arm of my coat. Still no gloves and no scraper. I sat in the warming car waiting for the front and rear defrosters to clear the ice and for my frozen hands to regain feeling. Last night's depression hung on me like a bad headache. It helped not a bit that it was still dark out. The cars along the street looked like mounds of snow. A lot of people wiser than me would be sheltering in place. I found myself wishing I had never come back from California.

I turned on the radio and the weather report on WBBM didn't help my mood. A winter storm warning, with high winds expected, had been issued for all of Cook County.

"Brace yourselves for thirteen to sixteen inches by tomorrow afternoon," the newsman said with apparent relish, as if it were a storm of his own making. A bright flash lit the street and a loud boom broke the stillness. Thundersnow, a bad sign for sure. I threw the car into gear, rocked my spinning tires until they caught, and began the slow drive to the coffee shop, wondering if it would even be open.

I parked my car in the one plowed lot I could find and had to endure a ten-minute gloveless walk in the cold. When I opened the shop door a blast of air, mercifully hot and dry, hit me along with the rich scent of brewing coffee. Inside the shop it was business as usual. The place seemed crowded for a Saturday morning. The servers were all bright-eyed, young, and cheerful to a fault.

I spied Kelley sitting in the back corner away from the tables in a stuffed wingback chair. It never once crossed my mind that the snow would keep her from coming. She nodded when our eyes met and I walked over to join her.

A waitress appeared before I could even say hello. "Big," I said, miming a giant coffee cup. "Cream, no sugar. And two chocolate croissants."

I pointed inquiringly at Kelley and she said, "Sure."

"Three then," I said. Kelley had both hands wrapped around her mug, like she was trying to keep warm. "And top her off, huh?"

"Thanks, Cosmo. You're too kind." Her voice was flat and expressionless. She must have had a night like mine.

With our backs to the wall we both watched the great flakes of snow tapping against the window. A large blue city plow finally scraped loudly down Southport.

"He's fighting a losing battle," Kelley said.

"Aren't we all?"

She scoffed lightly. In her big wingback chair she looked so small and vulnerable and wounded. It made my heart ache. "So...?" I let the word trail.

She didn't respond at first, seemed to be composing what she wanted to say to me. Instead she kept staring out the window until the coffee and the pastries arrived on a delicate china plate.

I figured the best I could do was wait until she wanted to talk. I took a sip of some of the best coffee I ever tasted outside Peggy's kitchen. Kelley turned her attention to one of the croissants with sudden appetite. She grabbed one from the plate and devoured it in three quick bites, like a person who has not eaten for days. Then she washed it all down neatly with a half cup of her coffee.

"That was just what the doctor ordered," were the first words she had spoken in five minutes. She seemed almost to fold back into the chair, like a child shying from strangers.

"Cosmo, sometimes I get what Mom used to call 'intuitions.' She had them too. Did she ever let you in on them?"

"She always read me like a dime novel. Didn't make her a psychic."

"I've got one now that scares the bejesus out of me."

"We've all been through a lot. It's natural to worry. It doesn't mean something terrible is going to happen."

"I don't want to believe Andy got himself so deeply involved in all this." She shuddered when she spoke his name. "But I know he is. Rules were always for other people. That's how he was raised. So sure of his own specialness. His own invulnerability. He got away with everything all his life. But he's not going to get away with this. Cosmo, something terrible is going to happen to him. It's just a question of what kind of terrible."

My cell phone rang. The opening chords of "Pomp and Circumstance" told me it was Don. "Do you know how to get in touch with Kelley?"

"Reaching out with my right hand would work pretty good. We're having a cup of joe at Julius Meinl's."

"Thank God. As soon as you can, no matter how bad the storm, get her to the rectory of St. Josaphat on Southport and Belden. There's been a development I can't discuss on the phone. There's a lot next to the park behind the church. You'll see a red door at the back of the rectory. Tom and I will be waiting for you. And Cosmo, keep her from playing the radio."

Kelley looked at me curiously as I closed the call.

"Slight change of plans. It was Don. Very cryptic, but wants us to join him and Tom right away."

She stood up. "See, something terrible *is* going to happen: I'm going to have to ride in your car while you drive in this mess."

I think we both shuddered as we trudged out of the coffee shop into the cold of a Chicago winter that would not end.

CHAPTER TWENTY-SIX

On a normal day the drive we had to make would take less than fifteen minutes. But this was not going to be a normal day on so many levels. First on Ashland and then on Fullerton all we saw were the blue city snow plows, busses that were mostly empty, pickup trucks sporting their own plows, their drivers facing a long and profitable day and night, and SUV's, lots of them, getting to use their four-wheel drive as it was intended for a change. Most streets showed only one rutted lane in each direction. I prayed that the car wouldn't get stuck or slammed into. Kelley had gotten quiet again. I looked over at her and could see that she had closed her eyes. Who's to say whether it was her feelings of dread or her fear of my driving?

With four balding tires, my sedan handled like a hockey puck, and driving that short distance required my full attention until the moment we spun up the incline to the church's plowed but nearly vacant parking lot. The few cars that were parked there stood like a village of igloos across the lot. The red door Don mentioned stood at the top of a set of steps off the lot. We put our heads down and aimed for it. The steps had not been shoveled in hours and the snow drifted and sagged across them. We pushed our way to the top and entered the unlocked door. We found ourselves in the middle of what looked to be a large meeting room. Tom and Don looked up. There were no welcoming smiles. They both stood up awkwardly. Don immediately came over to help Kelley brush the snow off her parka. Tom sat back down mechanically. He studiously avoided eye contact with either one of us. We stomped the snow from our feet and took off our coats. Not a word had been spoken by any of us. I braced myself for more bad news.

I surveyed the room. A near dead glass carafe of coffee, cream, a spent sugar bowl, and two empty mugs. The two men had been here a while. Tom's head was down. Don stared into his mug like he would find the words he needed to say in there somewhere. Kelley's eyes were half-closed and her teeth clenched like she was waiting to be blindsided. I swear I could hear the snowflakes falling outside.

"What happened?" Kelley said. "I have a feeling that I already know."

Don pushed himself out of his chair and sat in the empty one next to her and gently put his arms around her like a kindly old uncle. He spoke to her in a soft voice, almost a whisper.

"Andy is dead. He was found by his wife Marie this morning, hanging from a beam in their garage. He told her he'd be working late and she went to bed last night thinking everything was fine. This morning she was surprised to see his car in the driveway, covered with snow. It had been there for a few hours at least."

"No! I can't...I don't believe it." Her voice rose. She was angry. "He could have never found the nerve to do something like that." Her tone was even harder than her words. Don, wisely, didn't try to disagree, but held her and let her vent.

"I was the first officer on the scene," Tom said. "I had a chance to inspect the body. There is no doubt he died by hanging. The petechial hemorrhages, the drool, the ligature marks, all very consistent with hanging. Some other stuff Kelley doesn't need to hear. But the hair on his forearms was all stripped away at the wrist."

"Meaning what?" Kelley said, her voice catching.

"Meaning somebody had duct-taped them together," I said, "and tore the tape off when their business with him was done."

"The sons-of-bitches that did it stood there and waited while he twitched…like they were waiting for a friggin' bus," Tom said. He brushed a thick hand across his face before he could go on. "It had to take at least four minutes." He took a breath. It was almost a sob.

Kelley's voice was empty of emotion when she broke the silence that followed. "And just who would those sons-of-bitches be?"

Don looked grim. He brought his arm down from her shoulder and placed both of his hands palm down on the table. I noticed his wedding band. "There's something else. The supposed suicide came complete with a footstool, overturned to look like he had jumped off it."

Tom picked up the narrative. "One more thing seems to have been put in his car for our benefit. Take a look at what I found." He pulled a small bible from his sport coat pocket. "No one else has seen this. It was on the passenger's seat with a bookmark where a single leaf had been torn out."

Kelley put her hand over Don's on the table. "That means that someone is onto us."

Don looked at her and then over at me. "I think Andy's murder was an act of desperation. Somebody is cleaning up all their loose ends and probably hoping to scare us into silence."

"How could whoever did this know about your setting up the stools and the bibles? That was all inside stuff."

"I think at the end Andy had it pretty well put together," Tom said, almost like he was thinking out loud. "He could have spilled his guts. Maybe just to show what a good little soldier he could be. Maybe under pressure. We had him pegged as the inquisitor in that house on Kenmore. He might have been the subject of the inquest."

I shook my head. "He would have been marked up. Somebody lost more than a little blood there. Isn't it more likely that one of the Knights swung over to Gallo's team? Maybe even some small fry, like at Mel's level."

"What you suggest just isn't possible," Don said. "We Knights, every one of us, would die for one another. Look, we all agreed that Andy was working too many angles on this. When McTighue's world started to fall apart, I think Andy got caught in his double cross. He played people off against one another one time too many."

"Waterman's suicide was the ultimate catalyst for all of it," Tom said. "Joey, McTighue, now Andy."

"No," I said, "The suspicion that Waterman's death was *not* a suicide is what caused the balloon to go up. The Knights' plan worked after all, just not the way you meant it to."

It may not have been the most popular idea in the room, but it was the one that resonated with truth. We all sat in troubled silence, thinking about the unintended consequences of well-meaning acts.

"So what do we do now?" Don said at last. "Is it over?"

"Oh, no," Kelley said. "It is not over, not by a long shot. We need to know, no, I need to know if Gallo had anything to do with Andy's death. And Joey's and even McTighue's. We owe them at least that much, don't you think?"

None of us wanted to admit it, but we knew that she was right. We had become entangled in a mess far greater than we ever intended. There was no way we could walk away from it now.

"And if he was involved, he's got to go down," Tom said.

CHAPTER TWENTY-SEVEN

'm going to the office," Kelley said.

"It's Saturday," I said.

"It's better than sitting home and not knowing how or what I should be feeling. And I'm way behind."

Don and I both offered her the same advice at the same time. "Be careful."

She brusquely brushed aside my offer of a ride. I pushed the chair back and got up. Kelley handed me my coat and I walked out with her into the still lot. I watched her walk away as her figure faded and then disappeared in the falling snow.

With nothing else to do now, I decided to ease my way back to my own office. I had to pay to park in the usually empty Century Mall garage. It was almost filled with regular street parkers who didn't want to get plowed in. The block walk to the office was brutal, with the snow still swirling down and sidewalks slick and treacherous from thawing and refreezing. I picked my way carefully down the sidewalk, flatfooted, thinking about Kelley walking to the El, hoping she had the right shoes for the job.

After my attempts to clean up after the intrusion, the place was no more of a mess than usual. I pushed a pile of folders and unpaid bills to one side of my desk and sat down heavily on my chair. The light that told me I had voice mail was blinking on my office phone. I had two messages, the most recent from Billy Gallo.

"Cosmo," he said, sounding almost affable, "how about joining me for lunch at my favorite little restaurant in Andersonville,

Pauline's on Ravenswood." The *bon homie* in his voice rang false. "Drive carefully," he added. "We don't want any more accidents, do we? One o'clock if that works for you, I'll be there regardless."

The second message was from Kelley. "Call me right away," she said. "Something's going on here."

She picked up on the first ring of her cell.

"Cosmo, thank God. There is some kind of confab going on in Gallo's office. He didn't expect me to be in. He confronted me as soon as I got in and ordered me to go home. He said cause of the weather, but he was very nervous about it. When I was walking out the door there was a black limo with like those smoked glass windows. I could see the driver but not the passengers. I hung around a minute to see if I could get a look at who got out, but the driver was paying attention to me and I looked like an idiot standing in the snow."

I was halfway out the door without my overcoat by the time she finished.

"Go home," I said. "Unless it's a very short meeting I should have time to get there before they leave."

"Maybe I should go back."

"And end up hanging from a ceiling light fixture? No. I've got this. Trust me. Just once." She didn't speak at all, just stayed silent on the other end of the line. "Don't worry," I said, a little hotly, "I haven't hit the bottle since breakfast." I hung up without waiting for a response.

When I got there, I circled the block around the Pastoral Center and spotted the limo on Rush, right by the corner, blocking the entry to the courtyard, with the engine idling. I noted the license number and drove past it to a vacant loading zone five or six spaces down the street. I angled my passenger side mirror so it centered on the sidewalk between the limo and the door. I could just make out the shape of the driver hunched at the wheel in my inside mirror. He switched on the wipers every couple minutes to keep the snow from clouding his windshield. My rear window defogger was just managing to keep up with the snow. I didn't think I would have long to wait. A police car turned down Rush but paid no more attention to the limo or to my car than to a pigeon in the park. After about fifteen minutes the door to the Pastoral Center opened and Billy Gallo ambled down the front steps with a black and white golf umbrella turned my way, into the wind. Between the umbrella and the great hulk of Billy Gallo, I could not see the person he was leading to the limo. Billy opened the door and whoever he had been meeting with, just one person, slid into the limo. Billy waved as the limo pulled out, shook the snow from his umbrella, and stepped back inside.

The limo turned my way and I hoped for a moment I might steal a glimpse of the passenger inside, but as it passed all I saw was the expressionless profile of the driver—who was actually wearing one of those silly chauffeur caps with the tiny bill and the button on top—and the long stretch of smoked glass windows behind him. The car drove past me down Rush, but before it got to East Chestnut the brake lights came on, then the backup lights. The car backed slowly down the street until the rear passenger door window was right next to me. I lowered my window and, as the limo's rear window rolled down, caught the eye of the lone passenger inside. When I say "the eye" I am not being figurative. Just the one. Because of the crimson eye patch, of course.

He held my gaze just a moment and said, "Simple is better, Cosmo. Simple is better."

He made a little shooing gesture, and the limo moved on down the street with the dark window rolling closed.

CHAPTER TWENTY-EIGHT

I had to Google directions to Pauline's, and drove up Ashland to Foster, then north onto Ravenswood. With Metra commuter trains running parallel to the street, Ravenswood gives you a feeling that you're not in Chicago any more. With few buildings taller than two or three stories, it has a more of a small town vibe, with wooded residential lots and small factories side by side, facing the track's elevated rail bed, a high mound of grass and shrubbery in the summer but barren and frozen today. Still, I found myself wondering how I had never heard of a restaurant so close to home. I saw why when I got there. The storefront is what one might kindly called unprepossessing, looking like the kind of diner you might find on a backwoods road in the Upper Peninsula. There weren't many of these cozy old joints left in the city. Walking inside, I couldn't help considering how unlike the pompous Billy Gallo the place was. But there he was, sitting alone at a four-top with a red-and-white-checkered tablecloth in a corner of the nearly empty back room where few could see us and no one could hear us.

He half stood out of his chair and waved imperiously, as if I could possibly miss him. I took a breath and started walking toward him. The unexpected tilt in the floor put me a little off balance, and I wavered a little, as if finding my sea legs. I sat down hard on a chair opposite him, relieved to get off my unsteady feet.

"Ahoy, matey."

He ignored my clumsy attempt at humor. "Cosmo. Thanks

for coming on such short notice."

I lifted the menu I found on my placemat, but Gallo grabbed it out of my hands and flipped to the breakfast page.

"Forget about lunch. It's breakfast you want to order here. I suggest the salmon omelet. And I won't let you out of here until you have sampled the twice-cooked potatoes with onions and peppers."

An old waitress who looked like she had spent too many years on her feet approached with two mugs of coffee and a pencil behind her ear. She took a pad from her apron and gave us an expectant look. I nodded to Gallo. "I guess I'm having what he's having." I hadn't come to fight about food.

"Mr. Gallo will be having the five-egg salmon omelet with potatoes, cooked crisp, buttered rye toast, and orange juice."

"Am I so predictable?" Gallo said to her.

"No juice for me," I said. "The rest is fine."

Gallo seemed in no hurry to get down to business, and I decided to let him roll. So we sat there like new best friends chatting about the weather and about getting tired of Chicago winters and sipping great coffee. I took the arrival of our food as an opportunity to move our conversation forward.

"Sorry about your son-in-law. You know I ran into him a few times investigating the Waterman case."

He bolted a large forkful of potatoes and washed them down with coffee.

"Cosmo, you are looking at a stunned man, a stunned father. He was like a son to me, and I am lost beyond words." My silent glare seemed to make him uncomfortable. He took a more delicate sip of coffee, his eyes glued to mine.

"You have to know that I had nothing to do with his death."

"Funny, Billy, I heard that he hanged himself in his garage."

"Okay, Grande, if this is the game you want to play, so be it." He pushed his plate aside, "Let me put it this way. You need to understand that I had absolutely nothing to do with his suicide, or Waterman's for that matter. These imputations have got to stop immediately. I won't stand for it. I have a family, a reputation…a legacy that I can't stand seeing besmirched."

He started to say something else but raised his hand as if in a gesture of self-restraint. He seemed weary, far beyond Chicago-winter weary. He wiped his mouth delicately with the napkin while he composed himself.

"Cosmo, I am going to retire. I am giving notice to the cardinal this afternoon. I plan on taking my family somewhere warm, somewhere far away from Chicago. I have a feeling this will be the last time you and I talk. I want to clear the air."

"I'm listening."

"I know Waterman was outraged that McTighue's intrigues kept him from returning to the priesthood. I know he hired you to get back at McTighue. He as much as told me that himself. And I doubt he told you that was why he hired you. I also know it was suicide. That final act of desperation was part of his plan all along. I was fully aware that McTighue's financial shenanigans were ready to be plastered all over the front page of the *Sun-Times*. You may already know it was *my* dream to build the new parochial center in Bridgeview that McTighue ruined. You surely do *not* know that I was the man who first came to realize the risk and expense he created. That I am the man who convinced the cardinal at last that the whole thing stunk to high heaven. I despised McTighue. But I had nothing to do with his so-called accident. But I will admit that I have everything to do with the sordid details of his operation being buried with him. I have had to cash in every chit I had with the people who handle the chits in this town. That's why I can't stay on. I've done my last deal. But I'd do it all again because it was the right thing to do. It's my final gift to the archdiocese."

"So who killed Andy?"

Billy was silent, and I thought he was going to ignore the question before I realized he was trying to compose himself enough to speak without breaking up.

"Andy killed himself. Perhaps not the way it appears. But it was certainly suicidal for him to play the game he played. He apparently gave assurances to some very dangerous people that, because of his relationship with me, he could keep the house of cards from falling apart. He assumed I could be co-opted. By him. He was sorely mistaken in that assumption."

"So you killed Andy."

His face tightened, but he finally drew his lips back in a semblance of a smile.

"Nice try, Cosmo. Like I said, Andy killed himself. We are all eventually accountable for what we have done. And for what we have left undone. No one understands that better than me."

"So why did you want to talk to me?"

"I want you to understand that I always did only what was best for the church. And I guess I want you to be my advocate. I have the power to avoid public disgrace, and have exercised it. But I can't stop the murmuring. I expect you can. I understand why Waterman picked you. You are a better man than you think. You're not a man to be pushed. Ultimately, you're a man who is to be believed. I may find you annoying, but I always believed what you said. You should now believe me. I always did only what I thought was right. Now you do what *you* think is right."

He stood and pulled way too much money out of a gold money clip and left it with the check on the table. Those were the last words I ever heard him speak.

CHAPTER TWENTY-NINE

Nothing of the truth about the whole mess ever made the papers. Whatever else you had to say about Billy Gallo, he was good at his job.

A cousin of Joey Greco, the closest family he had, asked to have his body cremated. No one came for his ashes, which stayed at the Ewald-Barlock undertakers on Southport, whose parking lot Joey used to plow. They may be there until this day, waiting for someone to pick up the tab.

Andy Morrissey was laid to his final rest in Mount Carmel Cemetery, to the agonized wail of police pipers on the coldest day of the year. His fellow officers decided to forgo the mandatory drunken wake for a fallen brother and just went their separate ways after the last bleat of the pipes. Or so I am told. I did not attend the funeral.

What was left of Bishop McTighue's charred body was placed quietly in the hold of Southwest Airlines Flight 66 to Tulsa. The esteemed bishop lay in state in a closed coffin in the cathedral there. A gaggle of Knights of Columbus held vigil around the clock until his revered remains could be interred with honor. Ashes to ashes.

———

I had a cup of coffee with Don Bruster, at his invitation, about a week after the excitement died down. He seemed to want to assure me that I had done well.

"Ultimately you did just what you set out to do," he told me. "Waterman asked you to see that the man responsible for his death got justice. Whether it was to be a fiery death or a public scandal and years of imprisonment doesn't really matter much. Does it?"

I wasn't at all sure that he was right, but really had no good answer. I'd had my fill of death this unrelenting winter.

"That's not why I asked to see you, though," Don said. "We had a curious phone call from an attorney representing an as yet unnamed client with extensive real estate holdings in Bridgeview. They made a proffer for sale at a fraction of market value. I think the diocese is going to take them up on it."

"Blackhawk North."

"Billy Gallo's shining city on the hill is gonna get built after all."

———

I was invited by the Waterman Foundation one morning a few weeks later to witness the affixing of a bronze plaque to the door of the massive marble Waterman family mausoleum that stood in Calvary Cemetery. The family sepulcher lay near the black wrought-iron fence along Sheridan Road and offered an impressive view of the steel-gray lake. Edward Damian Waterman's body already rested inside in a bronze casket. I offered my condolences to a few family members huddling in a bitter March wind.

"He was a fine man," I assured them. "I knew him for forty years."

The workman wasted no time riveting the brass plaque to the stone. He was gloveless and fumbled at his work from the cold. Nowhere did Father Edward Waterman's final resting place indicate that he had ever been ordained a priest, or that he would remain a priest forever, his enemies a footstool for his feet.

189

Kelley began to show up unexpectedly in those weeks following McTighue's death. I would be sitting alone, surrounded by dark thoughts and restless cats, and would answer a tap at the door to find her there with an armful of groceries. An hour later the apartment would be suffused with the aroma of baking bread or a hearty beef stew or simmering lasagna. For a few hours, on those nights, the condo smelled like a home. There was a sweet, melancholy air to our time together as she processed Andy's death and I confronted an accumulation of blessings in my life I ought not to have squandered.

"I've decided to leave my job at the Pastoral Center," she announced one Friday evening over a dinner of cheese ravioli. "It is time for me to move on."

"Move on where?"

"Cook County DA. Don arranged the interview. And it seems I came highly recommended by the Cook County Sheriff's newest investigator." Her smile told me I knew who that was.

"That old dog. He finally left the department?"

"Special Investigator Thomas Keystone. At about double what he was making on the force."

"You probably won't be doing all that bad yourself."

"There's more," she said, as if about to share a secret. Her eyes shone with the light of someone bearing really good news. "I'm looking into becoming a Mercy Associate. A lot of professional women are doing it these days."

"I have a lot of trouble imagining you as a nun."

"It's not like being a nun nun. I'll keep my regular job, live as a member of the laity, but commit myself to the Sisters of Mercy in a formal relationship. I just feel like I need to be part of something bigger than myself. Otherwise, what am I?"

"Your mother's daughter," I said. "What else could you be?

CHAPTER THIRTY

Winter at last began to release its icy grip on the city of Chicago, and the weight of all the death and dying began at last to release its equally chilling grip on my spirit. One morning in late March I sorted through my mail to find a letter with a real stamp on it. My name was crisply typed right on the envelope, old-fashioned style. The engraved return address was The Waterman Foundation, with a PO box number in Wilmette. I opened it very carefully with a butter knife I had swiped from The Bagel Restaurant down the block for just this purpose.

I didn't read the letter at first, just stared at the check that fell out of its folds, and ran my fingers over the embossed dollar amount, like a blind man reading in Braille the best news in the world: $400,000.

The letter formally thanked me and stated that the foundation hoped I would find the amount of the enclosed check adequate for the services for which the late Edward Waterman had contracted before his untimely death.

The left margin of the letter listed alphabetically the names of the Board of Directors of the Waterman Foundation. Billy Gallo's name fell just below that of the Honorable Deacon Don Bruster.

I called Don.

"$400,000?" I said. "Whiskey Tango Foxtrot?"

"Billy Gallo's idea," he said. "With a quick second from the new chancellor of the Archdiocese of Chicago."

"Who would that be?"

"You haven't seen today's paper, have you? You are speaking to him."

"Should I call you 'Your Eminence?'"

"Call me whatever you like, but deposit the check before they change their minds. We've put together a little dinner party tomorrow night to celebrate your success and Tom's new job."

"Who's we?"

"You, me, and Kelley. Kelley and me in that we organized it. You in that you are going to pay for it all. 6:30 at Filippo's on Clybourn. Everybody's coming. Even a few old classmates."

He hung up and I started to the cabinet for a celebratory glass of Jack, but stopped myself and brewed a pot of coffee with a few drops of almond oil in the grounds instead. While the aroma of fresh coffee filled the office I went to the window and threw it open and let in a breath of fresh air, balmy and spring-like, full of anticipation and promise and hope. I have been haunted all my life by grave doubts, but one thing I can say for certain: In Chicago, spring always comes at last, no matter how hard winter tries to hold on.

Other Books from In Extenso Press

AVAILABLE FROM BOOKSELLERS
OR FROM 800-397-2282 • INEXTENSOPRESS.COM
DISTRIBUTED EXCLUSIVELY BY ACTA PUBLICATIONS